Love's violent birth

"I know this much," he said, taking a step towards her. "If you were my sister, I should lay you across my knee, young woman."

"How dare you!" An angry flush stained her cheek, and she stepped back hastily, for fear he should think of putting his threat into execution.

He caught her by the arm.

"Kindly release me," she said, coldly.

"Damned if I will," he retorted, taking both her arms in his grasp. "Now you listen to me, young woman—"

She tore one arm free, and before he could make a move, dealt him a stinging slap on the face.

"You hell-cat!" He said between clenched teeth.

For a moment, she feared that he was about to retaliate in kind and flinched away from him. But he did not strike her; instead he crushed her to him in a fierce grip that seemed as if it would break every bone in her body. Then he tilted her chin roughly upwards, and pressed his mouth ruthlessly on hers . . .

Also by Alice Chetwynd Ley:

The Jewelled Snuffbox
The Georgian Rake
The Courting of Joanna
The Clandestine Betrothal
A Season at Brighton

Published by Ballantine Books

THE MASTER
and the
MAIDEN

by

Alice Chetwynd Ley

BALLANTINE BOOKS • NEW YORK

ISBN 0-345-25560-7-125

Manufactured in the United States of America

First Ballantine Books Edition: February 1977

PROLOGUE

February, 1812

AN EXPECTANT HUSH fell over the House of Lords as the young man rose, standing before the assembly a little awkwardly on account of his deformed leg. It was not usual in that Chamber for any particular attention to be paid to a Maiden Speech; experienced speakers, indeed, often found it difficult to obtain a hearing.

But the young man with the dark, brooding countenance and flashing eye was known to be a poet. In a few days' time his poem "Childe Harold" was to be produced by the publisher John Murray, and the knowing ones claimed that Murray had great expectations of the work. Curiosity silenced the House, if only momentarily.

"My lords," began Lord Byron. "The subject now submitted to your lordships for the first time, though new to the House, is not new to the country."

Lord Sidmouth nodded grimly. As Home Secretary it was certainly not new to him. During the past few months, he had been inundated with appeals from the north of England to do something to check the Luddite riots. If the House should see fit to pass the Bill at present under discussion, perhaps he might be able to expect a little peace.

"During the short time I recently passed in Nottingham," continued Lord Byron, "not twelve hours elapsed without some fresh act of violence; and on the day I left the county, I was informed that forty frames had been broken the preceding evening, as usual without resistance and without detection."

Sidmouth leaned towards his neighbour, Lord Liverpool.

"He talks of Nottingham, but the story's as bad now

1

from Yorkshire," he remarked in an undertone. "I had General Maitland with me yesterday—he's in command of the military in the West Riding. He drew a gloomy picture of disaffection up there—burnings, machine breakings, and the like. Manufacturers go in terror of their lives and property, and are constantly appealing to him for military help. He can't promise it, of course. Not enough men available, with most of 'em fighting in the Peninsula."

"What about the Militia?" queried Liverpool.

Sidmouth shook his head. "Can't rely on 'em in this affair—foot in both camps, most often. I see nothing else for it but to make this Bill law. The death penalty for machine breaking should deter even the boldest spirits, eh? What's your opinion?"

His neighbour nodded gravely. Like most other members, he had read the Report of the House's Secret Committee, "On the Disturbed State of Certain Counties," and was fully aware of the seriousness of the present situation. Perceval's Tory Government never allowed themselves to forget that it was only twenty years since the French revolution; it was not beyond the bounds of possibility that a similar rising might come about on this side of the Channel. The war with Napoleon had sent food up to famine prices, and lately even the weather had played enemy, ruining the harvests. The new inventions in machinery were replacing human labour at a time when already there was unemployment due to trade recessions. In the eyes of the Government, industrial England was a dry faggot waiting only for a spark.

They listened while Lord Byron described with undisguised contempt the ineffectual measures which had been taken by the authorities to deal with the recent disturbances in Nottingham.

"Wonder if he can suggest anything better?" muttered Liverpool impatiently. "These writer chaps are all the same—look how bitterly Sheridan opposed this Bill when it came up before the Commons—nothing constructive to offer in its place, though."

"Well, at least it sounds as though this one will be in favour of it," replied Sidmouth. "If he don't like what's being done already, presumably he'll support more stringent methods."

He yawned discreetly. He had been late to bed, and up at an unseasonable hour that morning on affairs of State. He allowed himself to slump forward a little on the bench, and closed his eyes. Words drifted over his nodding head.

He sat up again suddenly at a change in the note of the speaker's voice.

"These men," declaimed Lord Byron, in challenging tones, "are liable to conviction on the clearest evidence of the capital crime of—*poverty*; they have been nefariously guilty of lawfully begetting several children whom—thanks to the times! they are unable to maintain . . ." His voice rose accusingly. "You call these men a mob, desperate, dangerous and ignorant—but even a mob may be better reduced to reason by a mixture of conciliation and firmness than by additional irritation and redoubled penalties. Are we aware, my lords, of our obligation to the mob? It is the mob that labour in our fields, serve in our houses—that man your navy and recruit your army—that have enabled you to defy the world! And that can also defy *you* when neglect and calamity have driven them to despair! I have traversed the seat of war in the Peninsula; I have been in some of the worst oppressed provinces of Turkey; but never under the most despotic of infidel governments did I behold such squalid wretchedness as I have seen since my return into the very heart of a Christian country! And what are your remedies?"

An excited murmur ran round the House.

Lord Sidmouth groaned. This was all very well; no doubt it was in the true Byronic style, and it had certainly made an impression on the assembly. But could the poet suggest any practical alternative to the Frame-Breaking Bill? He listened carefully to what followed, in the hope of hearing something constructive, something that a hard-pressed government might do to check the disaffection and the violence. He soon realized that Lord Byron had not concerned himself with such matters; instead, he was intent upon exposing the injustice, treachery, and uselessness of the present proposals.

"When a proposal is made to emancipate or relieve," he sternly accused the House, "you hesitate, you deliberate for years; but a death Bill must be passed off hand, without a thought of the consequences! And if you do succeed in passing this Bill, if you do bring to justice these men meagre with famine, sullen with despair, careless of a life which your lordships are perhaps about to value at something less than the price of a stocking frame—if you do, I say you will still need two things to convict and condemn them; twelve butchers for a jury, and Jefferies for a judge!"

He sat down amid a startled silence. It broke, and an excited babble of voices filled the Chamber.

"What d'you think of that?" asked Lord Liverpool, nudging his neighbour.

Sidmouth pursed his lips. "Poetical, but nonsensical. Shouldn't think it will carry much weight with the majority of members."

"Tell you something though, Sidmouth," persisted the other, "if that young fellow's poem creates half as much stir, he may congratulate himself, what?"

His companion gave a moody, taciturn nod. At that moment a note was handed to him. He scanned its contents quickly, then rose and left the Chamber.

He entered an ante-room leading off the hall. A man was sitting there alone, wearing regimentals which bore the insignia of a General. He rose at Sidmouth's entrance, extending his hand in greeting.

"Didn't expect to see you again so soon, Maitland," said Lord Sidmouth, taking the outstretched hand. "You've found what you wanted, then?"

General Maitland nodded. "Three men—Government intelligence agents, they call themselves. Spies, in plain Army language. Their part will be to mingle with the workers in the West Riding, and try to get themselves sworn into this damned Luddite Brotherhood. I've posted them off straight away to Colonel Grey, who's stationed in Halifax. He tells me that he's already found a good opening for one of 'em, at least—seems he knows of a manufacturer up there who used to be an Army man himself, and who's willing to employ a spy in his mill. From what Grey tells me, it must be a welcome change to find a manufacturer who's prepared to stand out against these damned Luddites. They're all scared to death, and begging for military help."

"If only we could spare more troops for the disaffected areas——"

The General shook his head. "Hopeless, with the bulk of our men fighting in the Peninsula. However, if once we get our hands on the ringleaders, it shouldn't be difficult to quash this affair. I'm depending on these spies to help us with that."

"Do you know anything of this so-called General Ludd who's said to be the chief ringleader?"

General Maitland gave a short laugh. "There's no such man, m'lord. There is no national leader, thank God, though undoubtedly each locality has its own ringleaders. I'm told on good authority that the name Luddite derives from a Nottingham apprentice—one Ned Ludd—who broke a stocking frame in a fit of temper after having been whipped by his master for idleness. Hence all machine breakers are Luddites."

"But what about all the threatening letters I've been shown which were signed 'General Ludd'?"

"Yes, I've seen 'em, too; sent to manufacturers threatening action if they bring machines into the mill. They're sometimes signed 'General Snipshears' in the West Riding. It's all one." He shrugged forcefully. "There's no real General Ludd, but it's a convenient name for putting to an incriminating document."

"So you're satisfied that there is no central control of this movement?"

The General nodded emphatically. "Certain of it, m'lord. These are simply isolated local outbreaks. Admittedly, one serves to spur on another, but I'm confident that there's no organization on a national scale. Come to think of it, how could there be? These people have no money for campaigns, nor the freedom to move about the country at will. Half of 'em can't read or write. How can they achieve any co-ordination of effort?"

"I sincerely hope you're in the right of it," returned Lord Sidmouth with a frown. "I must confess that I shan't feel easy until we have some of these ringleaders safely behind bars. I don't know—three spies doesn't seem enough——"

"More would defeat the object by drawing attention to themselves. Colonel Grey is satisfied, m'lord. Leave it in his hands—he's a sound man."

"He's stationed in Halifax, you say? That's right in the seat of the West Riding troubles, at any rate. I tell you, Maitland——"

He broke off, as a knock sounded on the door.

In response to his summons, a clerk entered, and handed him a letter.

Lord Sidmouth dismissed the man with a nod, and broke the seal. For a moment, he read in silence, frowning heavily: then he threw the paper down on the table in disgust.

"More news from Yorkshire," he explained briefly. "Fresh outrages—two mills attacked near Leeds, shearing frames broken and extensive damage done to the premises. My God, will this kind of thing never end? A magistrate at Horbury is appealing to all manufacturers to get rid of their machines, so as not to incite riots. A *magistrate*, mark you, Maitland! If the law is to condone these outrages, then we're already living in a state of revolution! What say you?"

The General smiled grimly. "I, m'lord? I say, bide your time. We'll see who'll carry the day in the end, never fear."

1

The Road to Liversedge

IT HAD BEGUN to snow again when the coach reached
Huddersfield, and the bleak February daylight had long
since waned. Mary Lister alighted stiffly, her feet numb
with cold inside thin, shabby half-boots.

She waited patiently while the guard sorted through
the baggage, and presently handed her a worn carpet
bag. She flashed him the quick, warm smile which always succeeded in making hirelings forget that they
could expect no great pickings from this particular customer.

"Where will I get a conveyance for Liversedge?" she
asked pleasantly.

The guard, usually a sour man, checked an answering smile, and shook his head.

"Nowhere—not tonight, tha' won't, ma'am. There's
nowt taks t'road after dark."

The smile vanished, and a shade of alarm crossed
Miss Lister's face.

"But I must reach Liversedge tonight—already I am
overdue. I didn't anticipate being so long on the
road——"

"Nor me, ma'am. But in weather like this, we're
lucky to get through at all."

He turned to another passenger, pointedly, ignoring
her. She made a final appeal.

"Is there anyone you know in the town who might
be going that way tonight, and would be willing to take
a passenger?"

Busy with luggage, the guard shook his head, tersely
recommending her to inquire from the landlord of the
inn where they had stopped.

She turned away at that, unable to help a certain

sinking of spirits. It had been a long, cold journey, and she would have liked nothing better than to put up at the inn for tonight, and go on to Liversedge in the morning. The thought of a hot meal in the warm coffee-room was tempting, but she was bound to resist it. Already her slender purse had been depleted by the cost of extra meals for which she had not allowed when setting out: moreover, she was many hours late in keeping her appointment with her new employer. It was a bad beginning, she reflected with dismay; more especially as he had not seemed the kind of man to tolerate shortcomings, however excusable.

She recalled their brief interview of some weeks since, and a frown marred her normally pleasant expression. There had been something so very uncompromising about the dark, taciturn man who had towered above her, asking short questions which were always very much to the point. She had gained an impression of unyielding strength, and some other quality which was not quite so simple to define.

She dismissed the thought and entered the inn. She found the landlord among a group of travellers standing in the passage. He shook his head at her request.

"Not this time o' year, ma'am, and 'specially not in this weather." He ran a professional eye over her, noting the new green ribbons which made a brave attempt to revive last year's bonnet, the grey pelisse which was just a little rubbed at the cuffs. "Of course," he added doubtfully, "I can put thee up for t' night, if so be tha wants it."

Her answering smile was a little wistful. "I must reach Liversedge tonight if at all possible. Is there no means you can suggest?"

He expressed regret with pursed lips. He had no time to waste on a customer, however charming, who plainly would leave his house without purchasing more than a hot beverage.

He moved away from her into the taproom, and she was obliged to retrace her steps towards the door. Before she reached it, she heard quick footsteps behind her, and felt a light touch on her arm.

She turned, to find a man standing there. He was

dressed in a frayed suit of rough homespun, but the muffler tied about his neck was spotless.

"I heard thee askin' for anyone goin' to Liversedge," he began, in a low tone.

A flicker of hope crossed her expressive face. "Yes! Do you know of anyone going there tonight—now?"

"Hush!" He shook a warning finger and looked furtively behind him. "Happen I do—but it 'bain't a proper passenger vehicle—tha'll need to sit on t'floor an' it's none too clean, if tha's partic'lar."

Mary gave a short laugh and shook her head. "Not I—not at present! So long as I can get to Liversedge tonight——"

"Hush!" he admonished again.

"I am sorry." She looked puzzled but obediently lowered her voice. "But I don't quite see why——"

"Never mind why," he answered cryptically. "I'm not rightly supposed to tak' anyone up this journey. But a slip o' a lass like thee can't do no manner o' harm that I can see, an' I can't bear to think o' thee being stranded in this thievin' 'ole. What dost say? Will it suit?"

"Anything will." The warm smile lit her face. "You are very good, and I promise not to do any harm— though quite what harm I *could* do," she added, with a puzzled frown, "is more than I can guess."

"Happen I'll tell thee—when we're outside," he whispered, once more casting a quick glance behind him. "Please to follow me into t'yard, ma'am. T'waggons are out there. I'll settle thee in, then round up t' lads. We must make haste."

She nodded, and began to follow him, though not without some misgivings. He seemed a respectable enough working man, and she was willing to believe that his offer to take her to Liversedge had been prompted only by kindness: but she did not like the aura of mystery which he raised. However, her disposition was to seize opportunities when they came her way, and not to let herself be deterred by bogies of her no significance beyond the desire of a simple man to own imagining. These attempts at secrecy might have appear important in a stranger's eyes.

She shivered as they stepped out into the dark court-yard of the inn. The snow was falling thickly now; it crisped beneath their feet.

"Take care, ma'am," whispered her companion, taking her bag and her arm. "Don't tha slip, now."

She looked about her. The yard was at present deserted; she could see no sign of the waggons he had mentioned. The occasional stamp of an impatient hoof somewhere out of sight was the only sound to break the silence. She began to feel uneasy: perhaps she ought not to have trusted him. Yet it was difficult to see what he could hope to gain by abducting someone like herself, who evidently could not afford the price of a post chaise. Even as the doubt crossed her mind, they rounded a corner, and came upon two covered farm waggons standing one behind the other, close to the road. A lantern swung at the front of each vehicle, but its light served only to illumine the figure of the driver seated beneath it.

The man made no effort to attract the attention of either driver, but instead guided Mary noiselessly to the rear of the second waggon. He moved aside the tar-paulin covering, and tossed her carpet bag into the aperture. Then he turned towards her.

"I'll need to lift thee, ma'am. There's no steps, think on."

Her hesitation was only momentary. "Very well. But how shall I manage without a light?"

"True—tha might hurt thysen. Wait, I'll fetch one."

He left her side, to return quickly with one of the lanterns. This he placed inside the waggon.

"Now then, ma'am." He lifted her easily in his arms and set her down beside the lantern.

She looked about her curiously. She was standing in the only clear space that was left in the waggon: the rest of it was piled high with some kind of metal con-traptions. She stared at these for a moment, then turned to her companion.

"These things—what are they?" she asked.

He shook his head warningly and looked cautiously around the inn yard. It was still deserted: he seemed satisfied.

"Frames, ma'am." He leaned towards her, mouthing the word.

"Frames?" She was puzzled.

"Hush!" Once again he looked furtively about him. "Ay, shearing frames."

"But that still doesn't tell me what they are," she whispered back.

"Don't tha know? They're machines for croppin' t' cloth—they've caused all t'fuss in these parts."

"Fuss?"

"Where art from, then, lass?" he queried, unconsciously falling into the familiar mode of speech "Hast never heard tell o' t' shearin' frames—nor o' t' Ludds, neither?"

"Ludds—you mean the Luddites?" she asked, beginning to understand a little. "So these are the machines which they go about breaking? And you are taking them to some manufacturer?" She paused as he nodded. "Oh, well; in that case, I begin to see——"

"Ay." His voice was grim, though he still kept it low. "I reckoned tha might. We're fetching 'em by night for safety's sake. Maister Arkwright warned us not to do owt or say owt to draw attention to ourselves. That's why I thought twice about takin' thee up along o' us—but I've a daughter meself, an' didn't like to see thee stranded."

"You're very good. But did you say Mr. Arkwright? Would that be the owner of Liversedge Mill, by any chance?"

"It would that. Dost know 'im, then?"

"I do indeed. I'm going to his house as governess to his stepsister," explained Mary. "I ought to have arrived there this morning, but the stage coach was delayed. What kind of man is he? I mean," she added hastily, realizing the impropriety of this question, "do you suppose he will be very annoyed at the delay?"

"Never fear. Young maister's not one it's wise to cross, but he's a reasonable man at bottom. Most folks don't give him credit enough for his good points."

"Young?" queried Mary surprised. "But surely——"

"Happen he's not young by thy way o' thinkin'," answered the man. "But I worked for 'is father, sithee, an' knew Maister Will when he were a little lad." He stooped to lift the lantern from the floor "We must get on now. Tha'll have to manage without this, ma'am. Pull them sacks round thysen; they'll keep thee warm, and they bain't all that dirty, think on. Art snug, now?"

"Indeed, I am, thank you." She smiled gratefully. "It's so good of you to take me up, and I only hope you won't find yourself in trouble on my account. Perhaps your employer will not mind so much, as I am also one of his staff."

"Eh, lass, he should be glad—reight glad!" replied the other, as he settled the tarpaulin back into place. "I reckon Miss Caro will, at any rate—tha's a bit o' a change from yon Mouse who's just left."

"Mouse?" Mary repeated. "What——" But already he had gone: she heard his footsteps retreating.

She glanced around her, but all was dark save for the glimmer of light cast on the tarpaulin by the lantern at the front of the waggon. It was insufficient to illumine the interior, and she felt a moment's uneasiness. Suppose there should be rats?

She shivered in revulsion, then took herself sharply to task. There was no grain in the waggon, so she could dismiss that thought from her head; rats were not interested in shearing frames.

A shuddering lurch threw her violently against the side of the vehicle. She heard the slow clopping of hoofs, and realized that already they had started on their journey to Liversedge. She righted herself again, moving her carpet bag into position behind her so that she would have something soft to cushion her from any further knocks. She shivered again. It was cold in the waggon, though not so cold as it would be in the icy wind which had sprung up outside: at least the tarpaulin afforded some shelter from this. She pulled the sacking round her to help combat the draughts which crept under the covering. She felt suddenly weary. She had been travelling since first light with only two short breaks for snatched meals at a couple of the poorer inns on the road. At the last stop, the soup had been too greasy for her to swallow, while the mutton which

followed it had seemed to consist chiefly of fat and
gristle. She began to feel hungry, as well as tired.

At first, she suffered all the discomfort to be expected by one travelling in an unsprung vehicle on a
rough, snow-covered track full of pot-holes. Gradually,
however, fatigue and hunger combined to make her
forget the physical discomfort. She drifted into an
uneasy doze.

2

Attack

IT MUST HAVE been almost an hour later when she was
abruptly roused by the sharp application of brakes to
the waggon. The consequent jolt dislodged one of the
machines stacked behind her; it did not fall in her
direction, but the clatter served to bring her thoroughly
awake. She sat upright, realizing that the waggon had
stopped, and wondering why.

It was then that she became conscious of the uproar
which was in progress outside. Voices were raised
sharply in anger, shouting words which she strained
her ears to catch. As she listened, the dull thud of
blows was added to the shouting.

She jumped to her feet, her heart beating fast. What
could be wrong? Was there some argument about pay-
ment of tolls, or the reckless driving of a heedless trav-
eller on the road? It was not uncommon for un-
pleasantness to occur over such matters.

She groped for the tarpaulin, and managed to pull it
aside a little way. Then she leaned out of the waggon,
trying to see what was happening.

The icy air smote her face, making it tingle. The
night was moonless, but she could still discern the
gaunt, leafless shapes of trees at the roadside, and the
dark tracks made by the waggons in the thick snow

which stretched away behind them. There was no trace of any human figure here.

Judging by the sounds, she concluded that the commotion must be going on somewhere in the direction of the leading waggon. She hesitated, shivering a little, and wondering what to do. Should she climb out, and try to discover what was wrong? Or would it be wiser to stay here, and leave matters in the hands of the workman who had befriended her, and who had seemed to be a man of some authority and common sense?

She had almost decided on the latter course, when the noise ceased abruptly, as though cut off by a knife.

A sigh of relief escaped her; but it was checked at once as fresh sounds rent the brief silence. A series of wild, blood-curdling cries now broke out; there was a quick rush of many feet, followed by the hard ringing sound of hammers descending heavily upon iron.

She put her hand to her throat; her heart seemed to have lodged there, almost preventing her from breathing. She knew now what must be the cause of this terrifying uproar, which sounded for all the world like some gigantic blacksmith plying his trade.

It was—it must be—the Luddites; somehow they had discovered that these waggons were carrying shearing frames. They must have succeeded in overpowering Mr. Arkwright's men, and were now engaged in smashing the machines in the leading waggon. At any moment—perhaps this very moment—she could expect to see them here, where she was cowering.

The realization would have been enough to unnerve some females completely; it acted on Mary as a cold shower, bracing her nerves.

She knew it was unlikely that the attackers would give her anything but rough treatment; she did not mean to stay here and put it to the test.

With trembling hands, she picked up her bag and threw it out of the waggon, then she prepared to follow.

She found it difficult to do so unaided. Her long, clinging skirts hampered her in her attempt to throw one leg over the high, wooden back of the waggon;

moreover, she could find no way of fastening back the tarpaulin, which kept hindering her by flapping in her face. Every moment's delay heightened her sense of desperation: soon she was heedless of rents in her clothes, and scarcely felt the blood start from a gash in her leg caused by an unseen nail.

At last, dishevelled and panting, she was sprawling in the snow beside her carpet bag. She seized it by the handle, and fled towards the trees.

She knew that her footsteps would not be heard above the metallic din of hammers: the only risk was that someone might see her headlong flight. It was a risk she preferred to the certainty of discovery if she had remained in the waggon.

The road was not wide, and a short rush soon brought her to the trees. She plunged into them, panting, and at once realized with dismay how little cover they afforded in their bare, winter state. If she stayed here, it would be easy for anyone coming to this side of the road to spy her.

Desperately, she plunged onwards, stumbling over tree roots, and becoming entangled with brambles from which she tore herself free in near panic. Her breath was coming in great gasps now, and there was a tearing pain in her left side. Her steps became slower; when she stumbled, which was frequently, her recovery was less rapid.

At last, almost exhausted, she tripped once more over a bramble, and this time fell headlong into a holly bush.

For what seemed an age, she lay there, unable to move or think, drawing painful breaths. At last, her tumultuous heart-beats steadied a little, and she found the power of thoughts returning.

If she wriggled a little deeper into the midst of the holly bush, she would be safe from view. Its prickly leaves offered ample concealment. Slowly, she began to crawl under the low branches, holding her bag before her face as a shield from scratches.

Soon she was satisfied that no one could readily find her. With a deep gasp of relief, she ceased to struggle, and crouched within the shelter of the bush, listening, and slowly regaining her breath.

For some time longer the din continued. Once, she heard footsteps running on the road, and a sudden shout. She cowered down in her hiding place, her heart once more beginning to pound in her ears. Suppose they should come this way?

It was only for a moment, however, and then there was no sound but the thudding of hammers.

Her thoughts began to race furiously. What ought she to do now? She began to think of Mr. Arkwright's men, and to wonder how they were faring. She had no idea where help could be found, even if she dared to leave her present hiding place. Irksome though the inaction was to one of her temperament, there seemed no other sensible course than to remain in hiding. Presumably the Luddites would depart when their errand was accomplished, and she could then see what might be done to assist the man who had so readily come to her aid when she was stranded.

After what seemed hours, the tumult died away. There was a moment's quiet: then she heard voices calling one to another, the sound of hoofs and wheels upon the road, followed by a deep and lasting silence.

It seemed that the attackers must have gone; but she dared not leave her place of concealment until she was quite certain of this. She lingered there for what seemed an interminable space of time, fretting inwardly, yet still afraid to venture forth. At last, the silence of the night began to play upon her jagged nerves. Her keen imagination peopled the darkness with terrors as real as those through which she had recently passed. Come what may, she must find some human companionship.

She crept painfully out from the holly bush, and, grasping her bag firmly, made for the road. It was scarcely surprising to find that her legs were not quite steady.

As she emerged from the trees, she heard a hoarse shout.

"Ben! Jack! Will! Art there? Speak up, for God's sake!"

She recognized the voice with relief and turned in the direction of it. A moment later, a dark figure appeared before her out of the shadows.

"Who is it?" She was seized roughly, before she could utter a sound. "Speak up quick, afore I throttle thee."

"No—don't——"

She was released instantly.

"'Tis thee, lass—art safe—what did they do to thee? Don't fret—they've gone now."

Mary rubbed her throat. It felt tender. "I'm quite safe, except for a few scratches. I ran into the trees, and hid, when I heard all the commotion. What happened? Was it—was it the Luddites?"

"Ay. There must 'a been a dozen or more on 'em, and only four on us. They pulled a cart across t' road, so's we 'ad to get down and shift it. Then they was on us. I got a clout on t' nob, and don't remember nowt else, till just now. Help me to find t' other lads, wilt, lass? I've been shouting, but they don't answer."

"Perhaps they're by the waggons," suggested Mary.

"Happen they be, for them 'orses is uncommon quiet." He stared across the road to where the dark shapes of the waggons showed against the snow.

"T' lantern's gone from one of 'em," he stated, beginning to hurry across the road.

Mary followed close on his heels. As they reached the spot where the waggons stood, a figure came reeling out of the darkness towards them. Mary's companion ran forward and placed a supporting arm about it.

"Steady on, now. Which of ye—oh! 'tis thee, Jack Hartley."

"Ay, it is that, Nick, though I never felt less like mysen." He brushed his sleeve across his face. "My bloody 'ead's bleedin'," he stated, in matter-of-fact tones.

"Likely," was the laconic reply. "Hold on to t' waggon, lad, and I'll fetch t' lantern. Dost know where t'others be?"

"Will Oldroyd was with me when they set on us.

Can't say what 'appened to Ben; 'e was sitting beside thee, think on."

He groaned, and again wiped his face with his sleeve. The man called Nick left him for a moment, and returned with a lantern. An exclamation of dismay escaped Mary as the light fell upon Jack Hartley's bloodstained face.

"Who's that?" demanded Hartley, staring at her.

"Maister Arkwright's new governess," replied Nick, shortly, removing the muffler from his neck. "Here, lad—put this round thy nob. It'll keep t' blood out o' thy eyes."

"Let me," offered Mary, conquering her revulsion of the bloodstained face.

Jack Hartley shook his head. "Nay, ma'am. I reckon I'll manage."

"I'm off to look for t'other pair," said Nick. "Tha sees why t' 'orses are so quiet? They've put t' nosebags on 'em—crafty devils! Bide 'ere till I come back."

"Nay, I'm comin' too," insisted Hartley, winding the muffler clumsily about his head. "Happen tha'll need help."

He swung round to accompany the other man. Mary, not wishing to remain alone in the dark, went with them.

They circled the waggons slowly, searching the ground for any trace of their fellows.

"How dost reckon they found out?" demanded Jack Hartley, suddenly.

"T' Ludds? God knows, lad. But it don't 'elp matters to 'ave those in t' mill who hobnobs with 'em," returned Nick, meaningly.

Hartley turned on him fiercely. "If tha's takin' a dig at my brother Sam, Nick Bradley——"

"I am that, an' tha can like it or lump it," stated Bradley. "All those men from t' mill who go over to Jackson's croppin' shop to 'ear young John Booth readin' t' *Leeds Mercury*, don't do Maister Arkwright no service. There's Ludds go to them readings, as everyone knows——"

"Booth?" asked Mary. Fatigued as she was, this

name caught her attention. "Did you say John Booth—the Reverend James Booth's son?"

"Ay." Nick Bradley paused for a moment, and studied her face in the light of the lantern. "Dost know t' lad, ma'am?"

She nodded. "He's my cousin. While I am in Mr. Arkwright's employ I shall make my home at the Vicarage with my uncle."

"He's a good man, the Reverend," replied Bradley, slowly. "But that lad o' his———"

He paused; Mary quickly took up her cousin's defence.

"He, too, is good—none better," she said, firmly. "I haven't seen him for a few years, but I know that he was always thinking then of others rather than himself. He can't have changed so much. I'll not believe it."

"No, ma'am, he's not changed. T' lad means well, reight enough—but 'e keeps dangerous company."

Mary was about to ask for an explanation of this remark; but at that moment, they heard a shout from close at hand.

At once, the two men ran forward. Mary followed; when she came up with them, she saw that they had joined a third man, who was rubbing his head and muttering a string of colourful oaths. As she arrived, Nick Bradley stooped and held his lantern over a figure which lay sprawled in the snow.

"Hold thy noise, Will Oldroyd—there's a lady present, I'd have thee know." He turned the recumbent figure over with one hand, holding the lantern in the other. "Come on, now, Ben, lad———"

He broke off suddenly.

"What's up?" asked Jack Hartley, curiously. "Bain't he comin' to?"

"Perhaps you could try rubbing some snow on his temples," suggested Mary.

Nick Bradley removed the lantern quickly, so that it no longer illumined the staring eyes.

"Tak' more than snow, lass, I reckon," he said, grimly. "Poor chap's dead."

3

William Arkwright

THE MILL AT Liversedge was in darkness except for a solitary light which burned in the small office at the front of the long, low building. A man in his early thirties was sitting there, poring over a ledger. The yellow lamplight accentuated the darkness of his keen, shrewd eyes, and of the thick crop of hair which was brushed carelessly back from a high forehead. The deep frown which furrowed his brow gave him an irascible look; but it was the weight of responsibility rather than ill-temper which lent the grimness to William Arkwright's face.

He moved impatiently, passing a hand across his aching eyes. He laid aside the pen, and allowed his thoughts to wander for a moment back over the past.

Eight years ago, he had been a promising young Army officer without a care in the world. From the first, his father had determined that this only son of his should receive the education of a gentleman: William had been sent at an early age to a well-known Young Gentlemen's Academy in the south of England. His visits from school to his West Riding home had been short and infrequent; perhaps this was why the untimely death of his mother and his father's subsequent marriage to the present Mrs. Arkwright had been matters which seemed not to touch him acutely. The birth of his stepsister Caroline, which took place when he was eighteen years of age and newly commissioned to the Army, was yet another event which seemed remote from the realities of his life.

Six years later, this detachment from family affairs was brought to an abrupt conclusion by the sudden death of his father. He had come home for the funeral, little suspecting how things would be.

For a moment, a rebellious look darkened the older man's face as he recalled the interview which had taken place at that time with Benjamin Drew, his father's lawyer.

"So that's how it is, Master Will," Drew had said, drawing his lips into a thin line across his narrow face. "There's nothing left but a few hundred pounds as you see, and the finishing mill at Liversedge."

"But I don't understand." The younger William had almost stuttered the words. "What of the mill at Huddersfield, that was started by my grandfather? When did that go—and why? My father was always plump enough in the pocket—he's boasted of it to me a score of times—there wasn't a shrewder manufacturer in the West Riding, I'll take my oath on that——"

"True—none shrewder, in his time," admitted Drew, with a shake of his bald head. "But this war plays the devil with trade, as no doubt others will tell you. There have been serious reverses, and your father wasn't strong enough to grapple with them during the last few years——"

"Then why the devil did he never tell me—drop a hint of the way things were going? I've been spending pretty freely—I could have drawn in my horns a little, had I realized how things were."

"My dear boy, that was the last thing he wanted. He was proud of your commission, proud of your claim to be a gentleman——"

William Arkwright had interrupted here with one short, ungentlemanlike word, dropped in the stress of the moment.

"Well, what am I to do now?" he had asked. "I can't continue in the Army with my finances in their present state, that's certain."

"Quite right, Will. There's only one thing that I can see for you to do," the lawyer had replied. "You must resign your commission, and take charge of Liversedge mill."

"Take charge—are you mad, sir? What do I know

of the textile trade—or of any trade, except soldiering, come to that?"

"Precious little, I grant you—but you can learn. And if you don't, Will," Drew said, gravely, "not only you, but your stepmother and stepsister will starve—ay, and your workmen and their families, too. For times are hard, my boy: make no mistake about it. It all depends on you, and what you can make of the mill."

William Arkwright moved impatiently, and took up his pen again. There was no profit in going back over the past; there was urgent work here and now for him to do.

During the ensuing quarter of an hour, the pen scratched away industriously. Presently, he raised his head, listening. He fancied he had heard a sound outside. He waited for a moment. This time he heard an unmistakable rattle at the side door.

He threw down his pen, and, striding quickly from the office, crossed the cold, stone passage outside. He turned up a lamp which was hanging on the wall, drew the bolts back from the door, and flung it open.

A girl of about fourteen was standing on the threshold. She held a storm lantern aloft in one hand, while with the other, she clutched about her a snow spattered cloak. The lantern's rays showed a small face framed by black, curling hair, and a pair of dark, lively eyes, very like his own.

"Caro!" His tone showed annoyance. "What are you doing here—and alone, too? Haven't I told you to keep away from the mill?"

"Don't be cross, Will." She skipped inside with that quick, eager vitality that was so much a part of her. She set down the lantern, and took his arm, looking appealingly up into his face. "Nell was coming with me but I persuaded her not to—it's so silly—of course I'm all right on my own! I came to bring you a message."

"What kind of message?" he asked, still frowning.

"Colonel Grey has come, and wants to see you. And Miss Grey is with him—and, oh, Will—she's wearing the sweetest blue velvet pelisse, just the colour of her eyes, and one of those new bonnets with big droopy feathers——"

"Spare me your Ladies' Magazine Fashion Chat," he interrupted, the hint of a smile touching his mouth. "Didn't your Mama explain to the Colonel that I am occupied here, and suggest that he might walk over to see me?"

"N-no, not exactly," replied Caroline, doubtfully. "You know how it is with Mama, Will—she holds the Colonel in awe——"

He made an impatient movement. "Yes, yes, I dare say. But this isn't just a whim of mine—I have urgent business here tonight——"

He broke off, aware of having said more than he had intended.

"What is it?" asked Caro, eagerly. "Do tell me!"

He shook his head, frowning. She gave him a shrewd look.

"You're worried about something, aren't you, Will? It's no use to deny it—I know! What is it? Is it to do with the Luddites? Or is trade bad?"

"A young lady should know nothing of such matters," he said repressively.

"Stuff! Oh, I beg your pardon," as she saw his face change—"but, really, Will, I am not—nor ever want to be—*that* kind of young lady!"

"You are my sister, and will be and do everything that is proper," he stated grimly. "You will begin by promising me never again to venture out of doors after dark alone."

"We—ll, I'll try," she said, doubtfully.

He seized her in a firm grip, tilting up her chin compellingly with his strong, thin fingers.

"You will do as I say, madam."

The dark eyes grew serious. "Of course, I shall, Will—but there are times when you don't mean to do wrong things, and they just happen. You know—like an emergency, or someone else making you do them——"

He released her, and laughed. "You're a rogue, child, and would argue your way out of any scrape—or into it! Heaven help the man who marries you, for he'll have his hands full!"

She pulled a wry face. "I don't think of marriage," she said. "Perhaps I'll be an old maid, like the Mouse."

"I doubt it," he replied, looking down at her with tenderness in his eyes. "Poor Mouse, you did lead her a dance! You'll not do so with the new governess, or I'm much mistaken."

"What's she like?" asked Caro, eagerly.

"You ought to have met her for yourself by this," he replied, frowning again. "I hope the wretched female hasn't cried off because of the weather, or gone first to her uncle's house instead of coming here. The arrangement was that she should be with us by midday, and here it is close on nine o'clock."

"Perhaps the weather's delayed her. But what *is* she like? You haven't told me, yet."

"Like? I really can't say. She seemed capable enough—firm but pleasant with it——"

"Ugh!" exclaimed Caroline. "She sounds horrid! Is she *very* old?"

"As Methuselah," he assured her, solemnly.

She looked up quickly, and caught the twinkle in his eye. "Now you are joking! I shan't believe a word you say—I shall wait and see for myself."

"A capital plan," he approved. "But the Colonel is waiting. I wonder if I could chance leaving this place for a short while—after all, they may not turn up for hours yet——"

"Who? Are you expecting someone?"

"Curiosity, young lady, killed the cat. I'm expecting Nick Bradley, since you must know."

"But you can see him at any time during the day!" objected Caroline. "You had far rather come and see Miss Grey, Will, for I know you like her, and you don't see her so very often. She is pretty, isn't she?"

"Certainly," he agreed stolidly.

"Oh! In that tone of voice! But I know you admire her—you can't humdudgeon me—I've seen you looking at her sometimes——"

"Young woman!" He turned upon her, all the playfulness gone from his manner. "You become pert. We must try and see if Miss Lister can work a change in you. If not, we may need to consider sending you to school."

"Indeed, I beg your pardon, Will." She bowed her head contritely, veiling her eyes with dark, curling lashes. Her mouth trembled a little.

"Well, well," he said, testily, "there's no need to go off into a decline about it—just mind your tongue, and try to have a little more conduct." He reached down a top-coat from a peg behind the door, and shrugged his broad shoulders into it. "We'd best go, Caro."

He went into the office and, casting a quick glance round to assure himself that all was well, closed the ledger and extinguished the light. He returned to her side, turned down the lamp on the wall, and picked up the storm lantern.

"Come along," he said, drawing her arm through his. "And take off that Friday face of yours, miss. What brought it on—the thought of school?"

He slammed the door behind them, testing it to see that it was firmly closed, before taking the narrow, snow-covered path which led to the house.

Caroline shook her head. "No. I shouldn't at all mind going to school if only the teachers were not too strict. At times, I get tired of being on my own with only Mama and a governess for company."

"But that's only at this season," he objected. "You have playmates enough when the weather's good, and the days longer. All the same," he added thoughtfully, "it might be to your advantage to spend a few years in a seminary. I'll make some inquiries."

She flung her arms impetuously about him. "Oh, Will, you are so good! If only they could know how good and kind you really are——"

"They?" he queried, sharply. "Who, for instance?"

She hesitated. "Oh—oh, some of the people hereabouts," she said at last.

"I can only suppose you've been listening to the servants' gossip," he said, coldly. "I've warned you before that I won't have that."

"No, indeed, it's not the servants—you must know how much they think of you! But some of the workmen—they do not understand why you are obliged to turn men off—they think you are hard and unfeeling——"

"That will do." She was not used to hearing that tone in his voice. "You are not to concern yourself with the affairs of the mill. I thought I had made this plain."

"Yes, Will."

Seeing that he was seriously displeased, she wisely refrained from saying more, and they finished the remainder of the short walk to the house in silence.

They were admitted by Nell, the housekeeper, a plump, middle-aged woman with wispy, grey hair. Usually, she was smiling, but now she greeted her master with an apprehensive look.

"I thought you understood, Nellie," he began curtly, "that Miss Caroline is never to leave the house unattended."

She started to answer, but was cut short by Caroline herself, who eagerly leapt to her defence. "It was my fault, Will, as I've explained—oh, please don't be angry with Nell——"

The little face was eloquent with pleading. He turned, and gently touched her cheek with an admonitory finger.

"Very well: we'll say no more. But I shall not expect this to happen again."

He directed a sharp glance at the housekeeper as he spoke. She nodded, relieved at having escaped more serious censure, for she knew the rules quite well. Miss Caro was her stepbrother's most treasured possession, and must be guarded accordingly.

"Are my visitors in the parlour?" Arkwright asked, discarding his coat and tossing it towards her.

"Ay Maister." Nellie hesitated. "Mistress don't know about Miss Caro," she added, timidly.

"She shall not learn of it from me," he replied, helping Caroline out of her cloak. "But no more of it—understand?"

He did not wait for an answer, but strode over to the parlour door, and opened it, guiding Caroline before him into the room.

It was a comfortable apartment, furnished in a style that had been fashionable some thirty years before. Emerging from behind a Chinese screen which had been placed before the door as a guard against draughts, the newcomers moved towards the generous fire which was burning on the hearth.

A stocky gentleman who had been leaning against the mantleshelf in thoughtful contemplation of the glowing logs, turned at their approach. He nodded his iron-grey head in greeting.

" 'Evening, Arkwright. Devilish cold—sorry to fetch you over here, but there are one or two matters I wish to discuss with you."

"Just so, sir." William Arkwright turned towards a sofa, where Miss Grey was seated beside his stepmother. "Your servant, ma'am."

Lucinda Grey extended a small, white hand, which he was obliged to take. Brief though his bow was, it brought his eyes within range of her provocative glance. He withdrew from the encounter in good order, without any visible signs of damage. Caroline watched discreetly, an alert expression on her intelligent face: she fancied that Miss Grey showed just a trace of pique. As for Will—who could ever be certain of what *he* thought or felt?

"Your pardon, sir, but I mustn't stay long," Arkwright said, addressing the Colonel. "You'll no doubt recollect the business I mentioned when last I saw you? It's for tonight."

"My dear chap, why didn't you send a message? I'd have walked over to the mill. Shall we return there, now?"

Arkwright shook his head. "No matter, Colonel. I may well have an hour or so to wait, and it's a pity to drag you from a good hearth on a night like this." He turned to Mrs. Arkwright, whose plump fingers were hovering nervously over some netting. "You'll have sent for refreshment, no doubt, ma'am? The Colonel and I will take ours in the library."

"Can't we persuade you to stay here with us?" asked Miss Grey, with a reproachful glance from her deep blue eyes. "I do so dislike a hen party—do not you, ma'am? Tell them they can very well talk here!"

She turned for support to her companion on the sofa; but Mrs. Arkwright knew better than to argue with her strong-minded stepson, even if she had not viewed with relief the prospect of Colonel Grey's departure. She had an uneasy feeling that the Colonel considered that all females of her age were little better than half-wits. Once this notion had entered her head, it made her behave like one whenever she happened to be in his company. She was aware that her intellect was not her strongest point, but never did she show to so little advantage as when Colonel Grey paid them a visit.

She shook her head vehemently, so that her long earrings trembled.

"Nay, lass—I mean, ma'am—if the gentlemen have business to discuss——"

"Oh, business!" Lucinda Grey shrugged a slim, arrogant shoulder. "To be sure, that must come before everything."

Arkwright's gaze rested on her consideringly, but he did not speak as he moved towards the door.

"None of your tantrums, Lucy," admonished her father, teasingly. "I told you this wouldn't be a social call, but still you would come."

"A trifle indulged, I fear," he explained to Arkwright, as they crossed the hall to the library. "But, there, what can a fellow do when he's left with a female child on his hands? She was only eight when her mother died, and I had precious little understanding of children—or time to deal with 'em. I put her in charge of that Foster woman—good-hearted enough, but a fool, like most females of that age. It wasn't long before madam could twist Aunt Foster around her little finger. Lucy's no fool, I'll say that."

"I'm sure she's not, sir," replied Arkwright, opening the door and ushering his guest into the library. "Would you care to sit there?"

Colonel Grey took the armchair which was indicated, drawing it closer to the fire. He cast a shrewd look at his host from under his strongly-marked grey brows.

"No doubt about it, that girl of mine's a flirt. She likes men, and makes no bones about collecting a host of admirers wherever she goes. Means nothing by it, of course," he said meaningly. "Just a game; like lottery tickets—only not so tame."

Arkwright nodded, realizing that his unusual burst of confidence was not without purpose.

"Tell you the truth, that's why I brought her here," continued the Colonel. "Don't trust that Foster woman—like to keep an eye on the chit myself."

"And does Miss Grey like being in Halifax?" asked Arkwright, politely, refusing to be drawn.

The Colonel shook his head. "Doesn't think it a patch on York. She wouldn't, of course. Plenty going on there; balls, assemblies, masquerades—anything you can think of—plenty of beaux, too, and gossiping females. Lord, she carried on alarmingly about how she'd miss it all, when first I told her she was to come here with me for a few months."

"Yet even in Halifax one needn't live quite like a recluse, Colonel Grey."

"No fear of Lucy doing that anywhere. However, that's not what I came to see you about. Are you aware, Arkwright, that there's disaffection in your own mill?"

"Disaffection, sir?"

The Colonel nodded. "I had a report today from the intelligence agent stationed in your mill. It seems some of your men go over to Jackson's workshop to hear this young whatsisname—the clergyman's son?—reading aloud from the *Leeds Mercury*."

"Oh, that!" Arkwright's frown cleared. "My overseer has mentioned to me that one or two of the men do go to these readings—but I'd scarcely call that disaffection, Colonel."

"Then what would you call it, eh?" asked the Colonel, sharply. "We all know what a damned seditious rag that journal is. It carries full and lurid accounts of successful Luddite activity in other parts of the country. Personally, I am of the opinion that it's bound to incite its readers to similar acts of violence."

"Perhaps it might affect some in that way But not

my men, that I'll wager. I dare say it's curiosity that takes them over there, and nothing more sinister. You must understand, sir, that most of these men—and their fathers before them—have worked for my family as long as the Arkwrights have been in the textile business."

"Do you know the names of those who go?"

"No, but I'm certain Nick Bradley will." He paused. "Do you wish to know their names, Colonel?"

"No need for that—I have them here." Colonel Grey drew a paper from his pocket, and unfolded it. "Jonas Crowther and John Hirst are occasional visitors to the readings. The most frequent is a man named Samuel Hartley."

"Hartley." Arkwright frowned. "Yes, Nick told me that he was one who protested at the time when I took the spy McDonald into the mill. That says nothing, of course. Any man might resent the employment of one from what the workmen would consider foreign parts—especially as I had only just been obliged to turn off several local fellows through a depression in trade."

"I imagine," said Colonel Grey, with the hint of a sneer, "that you are master in your own manufactory, and may do as you please without accounting for it to your labourers."

"You would be in the right of it, Colonel. And yet—they have a point of view."

The Colonel coughed. "May I suggest that you bear those names in mind, nevertheless? And now—what about this crank who gives the readings? What can you tell me about him?"

"Young John Booth?" replied Arkwright, thoughtfully. "Yes, I suppose you could call him a crank—he's only nineteen, but he's very much taken up with the doctrines of Robert Owen."

"Of whom?"

"Robert Owen—a manufacturer in Scotland who believes in education for the workers, among other things."

"Good God! I tell you, Arkwright, it's no wonder we have all this trouble with the labouring classes, when there are so many cranks about who seem set on giving them ideas above their station in life. Is this fellow Booth a practising Luddite, do you suppose?"

Arkwright laughed shortly. "Most unlikely! If you knew him you'd realize that he was the last to have any stomach for violence—when he was younger, he'd taken many a thrashing from other lads for refusing to join in the more full-blooded forms of sport. He's as sensitive as a girl."

"Then it should be simple enough to influence him, and get a stop put to this business. I wonder at his father for permitting it—a man in holy orders cannot be anxious to see his son hobnobbing with labourers."

"That's because you don't know the Reverend's own story. He was once a cropper himself; the Vicar of Huddersfield happened to notice his scholarly disposition, and helped him to become ordained."

"Good God!" exclaimed the Colonel, again. "One does at least expect the clergy——"

He stopped, aware of being perilously close to a breach of civility.

Arkwright gave a dry smile. "I fear we're a rough lot in the north, Colonel Grey—not a true-blooded gentleman among us."

The Colonel began a halting reply; but it was drowned by a sudden outbreak of noise from outside the house.

Arkwright jumped to his feet, and strode across to the windows, which looked on to the drive. Unfastening the shutters, he drew them back and stood peering into the darkness outside. After a moment, the Colonel joined him.

They both turned from the window with a start as the door of the library was wrenched open, and a dishevelled figure lurched into the room without ceremony.

Arkwright strode forward with a startled oath. "Nick! Lord man, what ails you? Is all safely managed? Well, speak out, can't you?"

For a moment, Bradley struggled to obey; then he shook his head. His whole attitude was one of dejection.

"What's amiss?" repeated his master, sharply. "For God's sake, if there's anything wrong, out with it!"

"There's nowt reight, lad," Nick Bradley found his voice at last, hoarse and shaking. "T' machines is all finished—smashed to pieces by them damned Ludds—and poor ol' Ben Turner's finished, too, God rest 'im."

4

A Warning

"Good morning, Miss Lister. I trust you slept well? Please be seated."

Mary returned the greeting, but did not bother to answer the question. Four years as a governess had taught her that employers did not really wish to know how you did, or how you slept. She slipped into the chair which Mr. Arkwright indicated, and sat facing him across the desk. She reflected that he was grimmer of aspect than she had remembered from their first meeting: the dark eyes had a steely look, and his mouth and jaw were set as though his teeth were tightly clenched. She was conscious that she herself was not appearing at her best. The mirror in her bed-chamber had reflected a pair of dark-ringed brown eyes and an unusually pale face.

The man glanced keenly at her. "I see that you did not," he said abruptly. "Perhaps it would be surprising to find that you had been able to enjoy a good night's rest after your experiences of last night."

An involuntary shudder shook her. "No, I must confess that I slept very ill, sir."

"I am sorry." His tone expressed no sympathy. "You will, of course, be excused from your duties for a day or two, so that you may recover from the shock you've suffered."

"Thank you, sir, but that will not be necessary." Mary's tone was low, but firm. "I should prefer to begin at once, if you please."

The black brows shot up, and he nodded, as though in approval.

"Just so—although I must say that you look in remarkably little case for it. Instead, I suggest that you spend today and tomorrow with your relatives, and return here to take up your duties on Monday morning."

"If that is what you wish——"

"It is. I sent a message last night to your uncle, telling him of your safe arrival and that you would be with him at some time this morning. So that is settled. And now I have some questions to ask you, Miss Lister. I'm afraid I must take you back over the events of last night, painful though it may be to you." He leaned forward in his chair. "Can you help me at all in identifying any of the men who took part in this attack?"

She shook her head.

"Think carefully, ma'am. Anything may help—a mannerism, a tone of voice——"

"I don't think you quite understand, Mr. Arkwright. I was asleep when the attack began, concealed in the back of one of the waggons. As soon as I realized what was happening. I ran away. I heard a fearful uproar—shouting and hammering—but I saw no one at all."

"Are you telling me that no one noticed you, or tried to stop you?"

She nodded. "They attacked the leading vehicle first, and I was in the second one. By the time they must have reached it, I was safely hidden in the trees. I'm sorry—I can't help you at all, sir, for I never caught sight of the attackers."

"Then how did you know what all the noise was about?"

"Something that your man—Nick Bradley, I think he's called—something he said to me before we started on our journey. He told me that great secrecy was necessary, because if the Luddites knew what his cargo was, they would try to destroy it."

"He did, did he? It's a pity he couldn't hold his tongue. No doubt those d——" he paused—"those scoundrels found out about the business in just that kind of way—through someone talking out of turn. I'd have given Nick credit for more sense. He's been with my family all his life—he's my overseer in the mill."

"Please don't be vexed with him." She leaned forward, her brown eyes soft with pleading. "He was so kind—and I was tired, hungry, and would have been stranded in Huddersfield until the next day, without his help. I am sure you wouldn't wish him to suffer for yielding to a kindly impulse."

"Are you, Miss Lister?" he said, in a dry tone. "But then, you don't know me very well, yet, do you?"

She studied his expression for a moment, unsure of her ground.

"No, she admitted. "But I have no reason to suppose that you would do anyone an injustice."

"Let me tell you, ma'am," he said forcibly, "that I am prepared to ignore a good many high-sounding principles to find the men who smashed my machines and murdered poor Turner. You may not have thought of it, but he leaves a wife and family without a bread-winner."

Mary made an inarticulate sound. Once again, she saw the tragic scene of yesterday in vivid recollection.

"As for the machines," he continued, pushing back his chair and beginning to stride about the room, "they were bought with God knows how many sacrifices on the part of my family and myself, and would eventually have brought prosperity to the neighbourhood—if only those poor fools could see it. Fools, did I say? Lunatics—murderers—mad dogs who must be shot before they infect others with their madness!"

His tone was now so ferocious, and his look so forbidding, that she flinched involuntarily. He noticed it, and came back to his seat opposite her.

"Very well," he said, in a quieter tone. "I've no wish to alarm you, and you need have no fears for Nick. He's the one man I know I can trust of them all. But I must give you a warning, all the same, Miss Lister."

She started. "I, sir? What have I done?"

He shook his head. "Not you. The warning is for your cousin, John Booth. How long is it since you last saw him?"

An apprehensive look came into her face. "Two years, I believe. Why, Mr. Arkwright? You do not—surely you cannot think that he is in any way concerned with this?"

"I don't know." He frowned, and was silent for a few moments "Yesterday, I would have said that he is the last person to become involved with the Luddites—a gentle, sensitive boy with no more stomach for violence than a girl! But now—I'm not sure, and I'm taking no risks."

"There was something Nick Bradley told me about John," Mary said, hesitantly. "I didn't understand it at the time—something about reading a newspaper——"

"Yes. That's it—he's in the habit of reading aloud to a number of workmen who gather on a Saturday at one of the local workshops. The newspaper's the *Leeds Mercury*, and it carries full reports of Luddite activities. One or two of my own men go there, I know, but I thought no harm of that—until now."

"But I'm sure John would do nothing to hurt anyone," put in Mary, quickly. "As you say yourself, he is gentle and feels things so deeply—if anything, he feels too much for others. He can't have changed so greatly since last I saw him that he is prepared to encourage violence such as I saw yesterday——" She paused, and again she shuddered—"Indeed he can't. You must believe that, Mr. Arkwright—you must!"

She raised her voice on the last few sentences; her pale cheeks were flushed. For a moment, his glance lost some of its steely indifference.

"Your loyalty is very natural, and does you credit," he said, with more feeling than he had shown so far. "But do not forget, ma'am, that kind-hearted people can sometimes be worked upon by unscrupulous ones to further their own dishonourable ends. Their very humanity make them susceptible."

"That's possible," she replied, slowly. "It's more

likely than that John has turned Luddite. He always had notions of trying to better the lot of the working people——"

"Maybe he's not the only one, Miss Lister, though some of us haven't our heads stuck in Cloudland, as he evidently has. If he wants to better the lot of the workers, then he should see that they understand the benefits this new machinery can bring—more trade, more work, more money in their pockets! It's a long-term plan, of course—and like to be longer, if the mutton-heads persist in this obstructive policy of machine-breaking."

She hesitated for a moment, then looked up at him with a puzzled expression.

"Try as I will, I cannot really understand what all this is about," she confessed. "As you may remember, my home is in a country town, and there we have no such troubles. I've heard vague talk, of course, of the Luddites, and how they go about breaking the new machines which are being used in the textile trade; but I am not at all clear as to the reasons——"

"That part of it's simple," he said, interrupting her with a gesture of impatience. "The men hereabouts are mostly croppers—that's to say, they are concerned with one of the finishing processes in the making of cloth. Their business is to cut the nap off the cloth, and for this purpose they use a huge pair of shears. You will not be here long, ma'am, without noticing the callus which every cropper bears on his right hand—a trade mark of his craft." He broke off, and looked inquiringly at her. "You may have noticed it already, in Nick Bradley?"

"No, I don't think—wait, though; yes, now that you mention it, I did. It was after he had lifted me into the waggon. I wondered at the time how he had come to have such a nasty mark—it looked painful."

"Not nowadays, though it is always painful to acquire. But to return to your question—these machines are capable of working several pairs of shears at once and at greater speed than the most experienced cropper can manage. Only one man—nay, a boy—is needed to tend the machine, which does the work of four men."

"So that means, sir," said Mary, her eyes on his face, "that every machine you install in your mill will replace three workers."

He nodded. "Just so—oh, I know that there are bound to be hardships at first! But later, when the machines are helping manufacturers to produce a greater quantity of cloth in a shorter time than formerly, when our export trade isn't crippled by the present war—a great trade boom will come, you mark my words! Why, it isn't difficult to foresee a time when machinery will take all the drudgery out of the textile trade, and leave the workers leisure such as is only enjoyed now by the wealthy."

A great change came over his face during this speech; the dark eyes kindled with enthusiasm, and his mouth lost its grimness. Mary Lister realized with surprise that her employer was, after all, a handsome man: such a thought had never before entered her head. His animation encouraged her to answer him more freely than she might otherwise have done.

"But in the meantime, Mr. Arkwright, they will be without work and consequently without money. How will they contrive a living?"

He shook his head, and the light died out of his eyes.

"I don't know—I tell you I can't find all the answers. What I do know is that my own course is clear. Man finds new ways of achieving his ends, and we must march with the times. The machinery will be a benefit to both master and men—but when we make changes in human affairs there must always be a period of transition which will be uncomfortable for some."

"Yes," said Mary slowly. "Perhaps that is so. But I do see now why they smash the machines that take away their bread; I think I see, too, why John——"

She stopped abruptly, afraid of saying too much.

"I cannot be sure what his part in this affair may be," he interrupted, his mouth taking on its former grim line, "but I have spoken to you thus freely in the

hope that you will use any influence you may possess
over him. Try to show him something of my ultimate
purpose; tell him he'll do better to educate the croppers in the notion that these machines will one day
bring real prosperity to the West Riding."

"You have not spoken to him yourself, sir?" she
asked, hesitantly.

"Until today, I never took his activities seriously,"
he replied, frowning. "Well, perhaps that was my er-
ror." He broke off, and looked her over appraisingly;
without offence, but in a way which brought a faint
blush to her cheek. "I imagine he will yield to your
persuasions more readily than to mine—in any event, I
should most likely lose my temper with him. See what
you can do."

"I will certainly try, though I don't know yet that he
is in any way to blame," Mary said, slightly on the defensive.

"I have no wish," replied Arkwright, in a downright
tone, "to cause any distress to your uncle. He's a good
man, innocent in worldly affairs, and your cousin's his
only child. But if I find that young Jackstraw meddling
in dangerous matters I may need to take serious steps
to restrain him. And I shall—make no mistake about
that." His clenched fist came down upon the desk decisively. "For I mean to weed them out, root and
branch, every damned Luddite of them all—I swear
it."

She was silent. After a moment, he rose, and pulled
a frayed bell-rope that hung by the chimney-piece.

"If you find my language somewhat forceful," he
said, "you must realize that the occasion warrants it. I
am going to send you home to your uncle now: the
carriage will be waiting for you at the door in ten
minutes, if you can be ready."

5

The Marchers

MARY AWOKE WITH a start. Her whole body was tense, though her mind was still drugged by sleep. There had been something unpleasant in a dream—she had been frightened by the sound of tramping feet . . .

Suddenly, she sat bolt upright in bed. It had not been a dream, after all. Now she could hear the marchers quite plainly; they were advancing with steady, measured tread along the rough road that ran past the Vicarage. How many of them there might be, she could not guess; but they marched purposefully, relentlessly, as though they would never stop until everything that stood in their path had been crushed and trampled underfoot.

She shivered violently, then leapt out of bed. Her fingers groped around the unfamiliar bedside table until she found a tinder box, and was able to light her candle. Reaching for her dressing gown, she fastened it securely about her, and pushed her feet into the light sandals which she had worn earlier that evening.

The marching feet had drawn closer now; they must be passing the Vicarage. She moved across to the window, and, lifting the curtain a little, peered out. The wall surrounding the Vicarage was not as high as a man; she ought to be able to see the heads of the marchers above it.

To her chagrin, she found she could see nothing. After a moment, she pulled back the curtains, and, easing back the catch, quietly raised the window. Then she leaned out, a plait of warm brown hair swinging about her neck as she peered intently into the darkness.

A flurry of snow touched her face, and the icy air made her flinch. Gradually, shapes emerged out of the gloom. She could just discern the outlines of the tall elms which stood at intervals along the wall; behind them, shadows moved rhythmically to the beat of pounding feet. It was the marchers.

At once she drew back her head, and without stopping to close the window, hurriedly pulled the curtains across it. For a few moments she stood there, motionless, her heart beating unnaturally fast. How could she have been so reckless as to risk being seen by these men, whoever they were? After her recent terrifying experience, she was ready to believe that at any moment they might come pounding on the door of the Vicarage.

She almost jumped out of her skin as a low knock sounded on her bedroom door. In spite of the cold night, a prickle of perspiration started on her forehead.

"Mary!" She recognized her cousin's voice, although it was only a whisper. "Are you awake?"

For a moment, fear kept her from answering. Gradually, the wave of terror receded, to be followed by relief. She picked up her candle, and tiptoed across the room to open the door.

John Booth was standing outside. She noticed at once how pale his face was in the candlelight, and that his lips twitched nervously. She recognized this mannerism from past years; it had always been a sign that he was labouring under some strong emotion.

"What is it?" she asked, in a low tone.

"The light, cousin! Can you have forgotten what you were told earlier?"

She drew in her breath in dismay. Both her uncle and his housekeeper had warned her that she must not on any account show a light after ten o'clock at night. The Watch and Ward had strictly forbidden it, since the recent disturbance in the West Riding, and penalties for infringement were severe.

"Oh, John, I am sorry! How could I be so foolish? Here, take my candle, and I will close the window. I've already drawn the curtains."

He shook his head. "No, l-let me. I can find my w-way about the room in the dark—you do not know it w-well enough. You may hurt yourself."

She stepped out on to the landing, and waited there with the candle while he went into the darkened room, closing the door softly behind him. After a minute, he joined her.

"All's right and tight."

He stumbled over the words, as he had done before. She knew the symptoms of distress, and looked at him in concern.

"What's wrong, John? Why are you not abed? And who—who are they?"

She waved her arm vaguely in the direction of the front of the house.

He shook his head. "We mustn't talk here. My father isn't likely to wake up, but Mrs. Duckworth might. I'd best go."

When they had been younger and were visiting together, Mary had unconsciously fallen into the habit of treating John as one of her younger brothers. Two year's absence seemed to have made little difference in their relationship, for she found herself reverting to the role of elder sister, now.

"No, cousin," she said, decidedly. "I don't retire until I know what's troubling you."

He swallowed, and turned his head away for a moment.

"V-very well, if you will have it so. We c-could go down to the kitchen—there's a fire there, and—and no one w-will hear us."

"You go, then," said Mary, taking the candlestick from his loose grasp. "I'll follow presently, when I am dressed. Make a warm drink—some milk, or a hot posset, if you prefer."

She returned to the bedroom, set down the candle, and hurriedly flung on some clothes. Her hair she left in the thick plait which was her usual style for sleeping. Not more than five minutes had elapsed before she entered the warm kitchen.

She found her cousin sitting huddled over the fire, which he had blown up into a flame with the bellows. A small saucepan of milk was set on the hob, and two pewter mugs stood on the well-scrubbed deal table. She sat down, and glanced at the clock: the hands stood at twenty past two. She listened for a moment; the sound of marching had now quite died away.

"How did you come to see my light?" she asked, for by now she had had time to think of this. "You must have been out of doors."

He nodded. "I couldn't sleep—I t-took a turn or two in the g-garden."

"In this weather?"

"I didn't notice the weather. I was too—too——"

"Occupied with your thoughts?" she hazarded, in a gently quizzing tone. "Shall I give you a penny for them?"

"They'd not be worth it," he replied, bitterly.

She waited, hoping he might add something to this. After a time, he seemed to have settled into a brown study, his eyes fixed on the fire. The milk began to simmer in the saucepan; she rose, and, lifting it from the hob, carried it over to the waiting mugs.

"There you are," she said, handing him one, and returning to her chair with the other. "Drink it—it will do you good."

She watched for a moment while he obediently sipped the milk. He seemed scarcely aware of what he was doing.

"John," she said quietly, "who were those men out there? And where were they marching?"

"Best not to know, cousin—else, like me, you might know too much for your own good."

She started. "You don't mean—John, you surely can't be one of them—a—a Luddite?"

This remark roused him.

"No," he said, vehemently, "no! Not in spite of all George Mellor's persuasion, or my—my s-sympathy with their feelings! I've always refused to take the Luddite Oath—'twisting in', they call it——"

"Who is George Mellor?" asked Mary.

He looked frightened. "I sh-shouldn't have spoken the name—even if I'll have no p-part in their doings, I would not b-betray them——"

"You needn't fear on my account. I should be a poor creature indeed if I couldn't keep the confidences of my own flesh and blood."

"Mary, I know—I didn't mean—f-forgive me!" he said, wretchedly, leaning forward to place a hand over hers. "It's just that it's all so dangerous—for them, for you——"

"Tell me all about it, John. You know you can trust me—and I have a feeling that you are longing to be able to confide in somebody."

"That's t-true, Mary. Sometimes I feel I shall go mad with keeping it all to myself. But there was no one, until you came. Very well, I will try to tell you—but not enough to hurt you, for they are wild people, Mary, although most times they don't understand the harm they are doing. Most times——" He drew his hand away from hers, and distractedly pushed back a lock of fair hair that had fallen across his forehead—"b-but what about poor Ben Turner?"

She waited a moment, until his agitation died down a little.

"Tell me from the beginning," she prompted, quietly.

Her manner had its usual calming effect.

He leaned back in his chair, and sighed deeply. "Who knows what *is* the beginning? I suppose it all started with George asking me to read the newspaper for them—most of them can't read, you know, cousin. That isn't right; why shouldn't everyone learn to read, rich and poor alike?"

"It's difficult to see that reading would be of much use to working folk——" began Mary, wrinkling her forehead. This was a new idea to her.

He leaned forward eagerly, his thin, sensitive face alight with enthusiasm; she noticed that the stutter left his tongue as he spoke.

"There you go, you see—you, a governess! Even you can't see the need for educating the common people. Have you ever stopped to think how much of their misery, how many of their hardships, are due to ignorance and stupidity? Yet they are the salt of the earth—as Lord Byron said in that speech of his not long since—they have enabled this country to defy the world! Those of us who've been lucky enough to have received any kind of education ourselves ought to

make it our business to pass something on to these less
fortunate folk. It's a Christian duty——"

"I'm afraid I hadn't ever thought of it in that way,"
Mary answered slowly. "There seems no practical use
for reading and writing in the lives of, for instance, the
mill-workers. Such accomplishments wouldn't help
them to earn their bread; and they have little time to
read for pleasure."

"But we must change all that," said John, vehemently, "for it is wrong, Mary, wrong! Have you ever
heard of Robert Owen of New Lanark?"

She shook her head.

"He is a cotton manufacturer who believes that by
providing good conditions for his workers, he will benefit both them and his manufactory. You won't believe
what he's done there, cousin! He's built pleasant
houses in a kind of garden village, for his workers and
their families; he's set a limit to their hours of work—
no one in the New Lanark mills is forced to work
twelve or more hours a day, as is usual in other parts
of the country—and, to crown all, he's educating children and adults alike, but especially the children. How
I wish it were possible to see this done throughout the
length and breadth of England! That is my dream,
Mary."

She smiled sadly, touched by his eagerness.

"But—forgive me, John—it's not very likely to be
realized. This man whom you speak of sounds to me
uncommonly like a saint. I can't imagine Mr.
Arkwright, for instance, following his example."

"That's because he doesn't see. Arkwright has one
aim—to keep the mill going as best he can until the
time comes when there will be an expansion in trade.
He believes firmly that this will happen."

"Do you agree with him?"

He nodded. "I think I do. He's a shrewd man, although he came late to his trade. But it's in the
Arkwright blood—generations of them were in the textile trade. It's a pity that he's set up the backs of so
many people hereabouts."

"Why has he?" She finished the milk, and rose to
place her empty mug on the table.

"Chiefly by being obliged to turn off some of his men because of trade depressions: but also by his autocratic ways. He'll brook no question—Sam Hartley, one of his men, recently protested at the employment of a new man from another town, when there were local men who needed jobs. Sam all but lost his own job for it—Nick Bradley managed to save him, by the skin of his teeth. They—the Luddites—hate Arkwright, too. He's the only manufacturer in these parts who dares oppose them."

"And I admire him for that!" exclaimed Mary, warmly. "Why should he allow himself to be intimidated by a gang of bullies? For that is all they are!"

The anxious look came back into her cousin's face, and he began to stutter again.

"N-no. Not all—though they d-did m-murder poor Turner. Because of that, I've s-sworn not to do anything that brings me into c-contact with them again—though not all who come to hear the *Mercury* are Ludds, cousin, I'll tell you that." He broke off, and she could see that his forehead was damp with perspiration. "But I doubt very much if they'll let me go—there are things I've heard that could be a danger to them. George trusts me, and stands my friend with them as far as he is able, and he is in sort a leader——"

He stopped again, and cast an imploring look at her.

"I'm saying too much, Mary—I knew I would—you l-lead a chap on so, with your quiet understanding——"

"You have my promise," she reminded him.

"Perhaps you might not be able to keep it—perhaps——"

He stiffened in his seat. A low tapping had sounded on the window, which was securely shuttered from the inside. Mary, too, jumped, and stood staring in the direction of the noise.

The tapping was repeated. It sent a shiver of apprehension down her spine. John came reluctantly to his feet, his face working in agitation.

"It's them," he mouthed. "They—they've come for me! Save me, Mary, for God's sake!"

6

The Promise

SHE STARED AT him for a moment while the colour
ebbed from her face, and her knees felt oddly weak.
Presently, she rallied a little, her protective instincts
aroused by his abject terror.

"Take no notice," she whispered, catching his arm
in hers. "Whoever it is will most likely go away, if no
one answers."

He shook his head. "No—not if it's them. They—
they——"

He abandoned the struggle for words, and moved
towards the window, extending a shaking hand towards
the shutter.

"No, don't!" cried Mary, sharply.

"Must see—who it is," he gasped. "Might make—
disturbance——"

He unfastened the shutter and pulled it back. With
difficulty, Mary stifled a scream. A hideous caricature
of a face was pressed close to the window; the mouth
was a great gash, and the staring eyes looked straight
into hers.

"It's—all right," stammered her cousin, in evident
relief. "It's George——"

This information did nothing to reassure Mary.

"Don't let him in," she whispered. "Send him
away."

John shook his head. "He's my friend—he won't
harm us. I must see what he wants."

She saw it was useless to argue, and watched apprehensively while her cousin gestured to the apparition
outside. When he moved over to the back door, and
silently shot the bolts, she retreated to the far end of

46

the kitchen. She was afraid, yet determined to stand her ground.

The man who entered a moment later was big and muscular, with jet black hair. Mary saw at once why his face had appeared so horrible; it was smothered in soot, so that his eyes and mouth stood out in startling contrast.

He said nothing at first but strode to the window and closed the shutter. His movements put Mary in mind of a panther, silent but powerful. He turned on John who was bolting the back door.

"Who's this?" he growled, pointing at Mary.

"My cousin, Miss Lister."

George Mellor advanced across the room towards her. She backed slowly away from him, until she was touching the wall, and his blackened face was within inches of hers. She longed to cry out, but pride kept her silent, though she was trembling.

"Miss Lister, eh? Tha's t' governess up at Arkwright's, eh?"

Mary nodded, swallowing a lump in her throat. Then John came quickly across to her side, and took her hand in his, facing Mellor defiantly.

"You're not to frighten her, George. You've nothing to fear from her——"

"Tha's ower free wi' names, lad," replied the other, continuing to stare fixedly at Mary. "Well, Miss Lister, dost reckon tha'll know me again, if 'appens we should meet, eh?"

She shook her head, trying to find her voice. "No—the—soot disguises you——"

She was dismayed at the thin sound that came from her own lips, in marked contrast to the harsh, gutteral tones of Mellor's voice. She made a conscious effort to steady her breathing, telling herself that she must keep calm, for John's sake.

"Listen, lass." He seized her suddenly by her thick plait of hair, twisting it in his grasp so that the tears started to her eyes. He drew her closer, staring down into her face with the concentrated glare of a wild animal. "Tha'd better not know me, think on—not if tha wants to live an' do well. Bein' young Booth's cousin won't help none, if tha should forget. Think on, I warn thee."

She tried to appear calm, but her bosom rose and fell tumultuously, in betrayal of her effort. The grim, blackened face was so close to hers that she could detect the rough stubble beneath the thick covering of soot. Body and spirit flinched from the contact, but she managed to give no sign.

"George!" John took hold of the man, but it was as though a pygmy strove to move Colossus. "Leave Mary be, I say! She is as trustworthy as I am myself—you shall not hurt her—she is like a sister to me—she will never betray you!"

" 'Appen not." The big Mellor stared thoughtfully at his victim for a moment, then abruptly released his hold on her hair. "Best to mak' sure, though, eh? Get rid o' t' lass now. I've things to talk about."

"What kind of things?" asked John, apprehensively.

"Private things." Mellor's glance at Mary was significant. "Op off, lass."

Still trembling, she turned obediently towards the door; but stopped suddenly, halted by John's expression of helplessness.

"No!" she exclaimed, summoning all her resolution. "I'll not leave at your bidding—not until my cousin asks me to go."

Mellor laughed hoarsely. "Ho, so it's got spirit, 'as it? It's 'andsome, too—always a sign o' spunk when there's a dash o' red in t' hair——"

"You'll not insult my cousin, while I stand by," retorted John, turning pale.

Mellor laughed again, and clapped John heartily on the back so that the boy staggered and all but fell. "I'll not tak' on the both o' ye," he said, with rough good humour. "All right, let t' lass stay. It's nowt so secret, after all—though I'll thank thee, ma'am——" for a moment, the former grim expression returned to his face—"to keep them pretty lips o' thine shut, or else——"

Mary nodded, not trusting herself to answer this threat.

"There's something we want thee to do," said Mellor, ignoring Mary and talking to John.

"No!" John's lips trembled, but his voice was firm enough. "I've told you I'll have nothing more to do with any of you, after what happened to Ben Turner——"

"That was an accident," replied Mellor. "Dost reckon we aim to hurt our own folk? Don't be so daft, lad."

"Daft or not, I want no part in any of it from now on," continued John, a note of rising hysteria in his voice. "I can't altogether clear my conscience of some complicity in that poor fellow's murder—yet God knows all I've done so far has been innocent enough!"

"Tha talks like a loon," Mellor said, contemptuously. "Why tha' didn't even know about t' attack on t' waggons, leave alone——"

"You don't understand—a man can be guilty of a crime without actually taking part in it—or even knowing of it——"

"Pah! Tha rattles that brain-box o' thine too 'ard. What I do understand is that soon tha'll need to mak' up thy mind which side o' t' fence tha's on. Won't be long afore them as bain't with us'll be reckoned agin us. Tha'd better be twisted in, lad, and have done."

"No—never! I'll not swear to aid and abet deeds of violence!"

John was almost shouting now. Mary started towards him, but stopped as Mellor took his arm.

"Easy now," he said, not unkindly. "Tha'll rouse t' household."

"Don't you think," said Mary, grasping her courage firmly, "that you'd better be going? It's late—my cousin is overwrought——"

"Hold tha tongue, or get out," Mellor said, without venom. "This bain't for women." He turned once more to John. "There's no harm in what we want thee to do, lad. It's about Sam Hartley, see?"

John shook his head, not understanding.

"Arkwright's given him t' push this morning," explained Mellor. "Tha knows Sam's no 'ope o' finding work hereabouts, and 'im wi' a family o' five already, and another expected any day. We reckon we'll not stand for it, see? If anyone's turned off, it should be yon chap from Manchester—he was last to come, and he's a foreigner besides——"

He looked at John, but the boy said nothing.

"T' lads are goin' to see Arkwright about it," continued Mellor. "But they'll need a leader—someone eddicated, who can fathom 'is way of talking, an' find t' reight answers. For 'e's sharp, is Arkwright—give t' devil 'is due . . . what dost say, Jack? Art willing?"

John still hesitated. Mary opened her lips to say something, but checked as Mellor gave her a hard look.

"Why—why not ask Nick Bradley?" John said, at last. "He's got—got influence with Arkwright——"

George Mellor spat expressively. "Nick Bradley! Tha knows full well he'll do nowt agin 'young Maister', as he calls 'im. We've tried Bradley already—he told us as Arkwright knows 'is own business best. Nay, lad, there's nobbut thysen, for tha'rt only chap can stand up to yon fiend in argument—an' that's what we mean to try—at first." He clapped John on the back with what was intended as encouragement. "Come on, now, look sharp—I haven't all night—wilt do it?"

"I think," said Mary, speaking very slowly and carefully so that she might not betray her nervousness, "it would be a bad time to undertake such a venture. Mr. Arkwright told—told me this morning——" she swallowed as Mellor stared at her—"he gave me a warning for John. If he finds him meddling, he said, in dangerous matters——"

"Ay," interrupted Mellor fiercely, taking a step towards her. "Ay—what'll he do?"

"He—didn't say—precisely—but he did say that he was determined——"

She stopped, conscious that what she was about to say might serve to inflame the black giant.

"Do I have to shake it out o' thee?" threatened Mellor, advancing.

She clenched her hands to still their trembling. "No. But you won't like it. He said he meant to weed out all the Luddites, root and branch."

To her relief, the giant threw back his head and laughed. "He did, eh? It'd tak' more than Arkwright, I reckon! We're a match for 'im, never fear. We'll see 'ow he deals wi' us ower this business—then let 'im look out, that's all!"

"I think—he means well——" ventured Mary, encouraged by his good humour.

" 'Appen t' devil means well, too—it's actions, not thoughts, as mak's or mar's folks's lives," returned Mellor, gruffly. "But I've no time to stand in idle chat wi' thee, lass. Art goin' with t' lads then, Jack?"

"Who else is going?" asked John, hesitantly.

"Only Arkwright's men—oh, ay, we're none so daft as to send outsiders. There'll be half a dozen on 'em, includin' Sam's brother Jack—who's no friend o' ours, as tha knows well, but who won't see 'is own brother starve for lack o' askin for 'is job back. We couldn't get more support—t' others be in Arkwright's pocket, an' a lily-livered set o' swine besides. Reckon they'll all come to see it our way fast enough, one day. We'll bide our time."

"Then it will be—just a peaceable deputation of some of Arkwright's own workmen?" asked John. "And simply to ask—beg—Arkwright to give Sam Hartley back his job for the sake of his wife and family? No more? No—no threats of violence, or—or——"

His sensitive face worked as his mind turned swiftly back to Ben Turner's death.

"Ay; tha's hit t' nail on t' head," replied Mellor, watching him. "Well? What dost say?"

"There seems no harm," said John, slowly. "Poor Sam—there's nothing hereabouts for him, I well know. He might get agricultural work in the summer—but he's got to live until then, and a young family at that."

He paused, thinking. In the uneasy silence, Mary was unreasonably conscious of the ticking of the grandfather clock which stood against one wall. She wanted to rush over to John, and urge him not to have any part in the scheme. Fear of the giant, great though it was, would not by itself have deterred her; but in her heart she knew that this youth, though both sensitive and timid, could never be deflected from what he considered to be his duty. Alone with her, he might have yielded to her persuasions as to where that duty lay: with Mellor present, there could be only one outcome.

"That's fixed, then." Mellor showed little sign of the satisfaction he was feeling; instead, he treated John's assent as if he had expected it. "They're meeting outside t' mill at three o'clock tomorrow—or today, whichever way tha looks on 'it. They'll go straight up to Arkwright's 'ouse."

"On the Sabbath?" asked John, wonderingly.

"Better t' day, better t' deed," Mellor answered, laconically. "'Tis only day they bain't at work, and only time they be certain o' catchin' Arkwright at 'ome."

Mary wondered how her employer would relish having his one day of rest interrupted, and tried to catch John's eye in warning. Mr. Arkwright had seemed to her to be neither a patient nor a particularly understanding man, in spite of the fact that Nick Bradley had spoken well of him. Moreover, he had warned Mary specifically against her cousin's meddling in matters of this kind.

It was useless, however. She could see that John was powerless to resist the appeal of a fellow creature in need.

Dismayed, she heard him give his word to George Mellor; and knew that nothing she could say thereafter—indeed, nothing on earth save death itself—would suffice to make him break it.

7

A Deputation to Mr. Arkwright

STANDING SILENTLY BESIDE her cousin and Mrs. Duckworth, the housekeeper, in the narrow, wooden pew, Mary glanced covertly around the little village church.

A fair-sized congregation was present, composed for the most part of croppers and their families. Their patient, submissive faces gave no hint of the feelings which had given rise to the violent happenings of the last few days. They stood quietly enough now, their work-worn hands gripping the rail in front of them as they waited for the service to begin.

She saw the Arkwright family approaching down the aisle, and she quickly turned her head to the front. They entered the opposite pew, so that she had ample opportunity to study them if she wished. Her glance lingered particularly on Caroline, whom so far she had not met. She liked what she saw: the eager, vital face promised intelligence, and there was warmth in the smile which the girl turned from time to time on her stepbrother. William Arkwright himself stood stiff and unsmiling beside Caroline and her mother, who was finely dressed in a fur-trimmed black velvet pelisse and an over-elaborate purple bonnet with ostrich plumes. Mrs. Arkwright looked plump, contented and of a different cast of mind from her young daughter. Mary hazarded a guess that if Mrs. Arkwright alone had been in charge of Caroline, the girl would have been sadly spoilt. She glanced again at her employer, and decided that as long as he kept the reins in his hands, there was little fear of such an outcome. Indeed, the trouble might be that some day the liveliness of the girl would run counter to her stepbrother's autocracy. Who would win, then, Mary wondered? Physically, they were much alike; but she had yet to discover if they shared the unyielding disposition which she had already noticed in William Arkwright.

Her uncle's sermon was commendably short, for he knew the difficulties of housewives who wished to do justice to the one meat dinner of the week which they could afford to put before their families. His exposition of the text from Corinthians "Be of one mind, live in peace" was scholarly, but made no reference to the recent violations of peace in the neighbourhood. He had always been an unworldly man, Mary reflected, and of course his deafness served to isolate him somewhat from the troubles around him; but surely he could not really be as unaware of them as he appeared to be? She glanced at John, sitting soberly beside her; and wondered if he, too, found his father's sermons out of touch with the harsh realities which surrounded them. In his father's place, could John have found words which would have whipped expression into the polite, blank faces of the congregation, and found an echo in their hearts?

She caught Mrs. Arkwright's eye upon her, and looked down at the hymn book which was clasped in her hands, a faint blush rising to her cheek.

The service over, they all filed slowly out of church into the cold, fitful sunshine, some standing for a while in small groups, idly chatting. Mrs. Duckworth was soon pounced upon by a neighbour, and Mary and John were left for a moment standing together in the middle of the path. She started to say something, but stopped as she noticed that his gaze was fixed in another direction. Her eyes followed his, until they came to rest on a figure standing at some distance away among the gravestones, half concealed from view by a dark yew.

Something in the build and stance of the figure made her catch her breath in sudden, unreasoning fear. She knew who this man was, although she could not recognize his face even had she been close enough to discern the features.

She felt John move, and put out her hand to stop him.

"No!" she whispered, urgently. "Don't go."

"I must, Mary," he replied, and shook her gently off.

He began to thread his way through the small groups which surrounded them. She started in pursuit, but had taken only a few steps when she felt a touch on her arm, and, turning, saw Mr. Arkwright there.

He bowed curtly. "Good morning, ma'am. I want you to make my sister's acquaintance."

She had no choice but to follow him down the path to the spot by the lych-gate where Mrs. Arkwright and Caroline were awaiting him. Mrs. Arkwright was deep in conversation with an acquaintance, but she detached herself as her stepson came up, and greeted Mary kindly, if somewhat effusively.

"Are you feeling more the thing today, Miss Lister? You looked properly poorly the other night, and no wonder, poor thing, after what you'd just been through—but you look much stouter today, I assure you, and I am very glad of it. I said to Will, 'That poor girl,' I said——"

"Caroline," interrupted Arkwright, "this is Miss Lister, your new governess."

"How d'you do, ma'am?"

The girl bobbed, and directed a quick, shy smile at Mary. Her lively eyes searched the governess's face, looking for some sign that they were to be friends. Mary tried to forget her sudden anxiety about John and the sinister figure in the churchyard. She gave an answering smile, charged with warmth and reassurance. She watched the slight tension die out of the girl's face as she gave her quiet response.

"I think you have something to ask Miss Lister," Arkwright prompted his stepmother, with a slight smile.

"I? Oh, yes, to be sure!" Mrs. Arkwright started, for she had been watching closely to see how her darling would receive the new governess. "Will thought—that is to say, I would very much like you to come and take a dish of tea with me this afternoon, if you are not doing anything else, you know. It would be a splendid opportunity for you and Caro to get to know each other, before you start your lessons together tomorrow, don't you agree, Miss Lister? Though I am sure you will go on famously; for the minute I set eyes on you I knew you would be more suitable than that Miss Mercer, who was a dear, good creature, poor soul, but so dreadfully prim, as though she had been at least a hundred years old, which Caro thought she most likely was!" She paused for breath, but was on again before anyone could stop her. "Though to be sure, I did wonder if perhaps you might not be just a bit too young for a governess—but Will thought you capable, and he's always right, you know——"

"You give me a depressing character," interrupted

William Arkwright, lightly. "What time would be convenient for you, Miss Lister?"

Mary hastily named three o'clock, and then wished
that she had not done so. She recollected only too well
that it was the hour appointed for the deputation to
meet at Liversedge mill. What perverse fate had made
her employer ask her to be at his house this afternoon?
Yet, in a way, she wanted to be close at hand when her
cousin paid his call.

She parted from the Arkwrights as soon as she
could, and, making her way back along the path,
started across the grass towards the spot where she had
seen the man standing. Little as she wished to meet
him again, she did not intend to leave John in his company. No one was there now: both he and her cousin
were gone.

Mary was admitted to Mr. Arkwright's house by
Nell, who automatically adjured her to wipe her feet,
then hastily apologized.

"Oh, I beg pardon, ma'am! But everyone's in and
out, and 'tis so dirty underfoot, now t' snow's
clearing."

"It is indeed," replied Mary. "I'd like to change my
boots for these slippers, if I may."

Nell ushered her into a small cloakroom on the
ground floor, and good naturedly helped her to remove
her half boots.

"There's company, besides yoursen," she gossiped.
"Pretty little Miss Grey's here with Miss Foster—they
came not much above a half hour since. You'll mind
seeing Miss Grey t' other night, when that awful
business happened—Maister Will's not going to get
over that in a hurry, mark my words. He's taking it
hard, poor lad."

The freedom of speech of the North country domestics always struck strangely on Mary's ears after a long
absence. Farther South, manners were more guarded;
but she warmed to the personal touch that always
greeted her in Yorkshire.

The housekeeper shepherded her along a passage

which led to the parlour, and, tapping on the door, announced her.

Mary walked into the room: she was not feeling completely at ease, which was only natural in the circumstances. Her feelings of diffidence were increased, however, by the sudden silence which greeted her arrival; and by the long, calculating stare bestowed on her by Miss Grey.

It was true that she had seen Lucinda Grey before, on the night of the Luddite attack; but she had then been too fatigued and upset to take much notice of her. Now, as her troubled brown eyes met the contemptuous blue ones across the room, she realized with a shock that here was one of the loveliest women she had ever known. The cherry red gown that Miss Grey was wearing accentuated her fair skin, and gave added lustre to her rich golden curls. She turned her head with a langorous movement, and Mary noticed that William Arkwright's eyes were reluctant to leave her face.

Mary was just beginning to feel decidedly uncomfortable when her employer rose, and came towards her, drawing her into the circle. Mrs. Arkwright, too, who had been busy picking up some dropped stitches in her work, sat up and gave her a friendly, if verbose, greeting.

"May I present Miss Lister?" said Arkwright to the others. "Miss Grey—Miss Foster."

Miss Foster managed a quiet "How d'ye do," but Lucinda Grey contented herself with a cool nod. Mary felt the colour rising in her cheeks, and despised herself for the weakness.

"Come, sit by Caro and let her entertain you," said Arkwright, setting a chair for her beside his stepsister. His tone was kinder than any he had so far used towards her, and she felt disproportionately grateful for it.

She began to talk to Caroline, and in her attempts to draw the girl out, soon forgot her own diffidence. After a while, they were chatting happily together as if they had known each other for years. Mary noticed presently that Mr. Arkwright had transferred his attention from Miss Grey for the time being, and was an interested listener to the conversation between Caroline and herself. This brought on a return of her former self-consciousness, and some of the spontaneity went out of her remarks.

"Show Miss Lister some of your drawings, Caro," suggested Arkwright, suddenly.

As the girl rose to obey, Mary glanced quickly at his face, trying to read its expression. Could she be mistaken, or had he noticed her shyness, and was trying to find a way to set her at ease again? She would not have judged him to be a man who was either perceptive or careful of the feelings of others. She did not know what to think, and his countenance told her nothing.

The sketches did the trick, however: in looking, commenting and occasionally laughing over them with Caroline, Mary quite recovered her poise.

When tea was brought in and conversation became general, the sketches were passed around.

"Do you draw, sir?" asked Miss Grey, turning towards Arkwright with one of her langorous movements.

He shook his head. "I received scant encouragement as a boy—the only portrait I ever executed was done in chalk on the blackboard. The subject—one of my masters—took an instant dislike to it. The memory of that early effort is so painful that I've never tried my hand at drawing since."

There was a general laugh at this.

"I should like to try a likeness of your sister and yourself," said Miss Grey, with the slight drawl which gave something of a sneer to all her remarks.

Arkwright bowed. "You honour us, ma'am; but I fear we should be poor subjects, though for different reasons; I rarely find time to sit still, and my sister is quite unable to do so."

Mary fancied that Miss Grey's lovely face showed signs of pique, but she shrugged carelessly.

"As you please, Mr. Arkwright. But all work and no play, you know——"

"That is just what I am always telling him!" interrupted Mrs. Arkwright, triumphantly. "He works day

and night without pause, and rarely stops for long
enough to eat his mutton with a neighbour, leave alone
take part in any of the evening parties and occasional
balls in the neighbourhood—for I would not have you
think, Miss Grey," she said, earnestly, turning to her
attractive neighbour, "that we don't have anything of
that kind hereabouts, just as much as you do in York!
Though, of course, we don't have Assemblies, exactly,
but still——"

"It's no good, ma'am," interrupted Arkwright, seeing
the boredom in Lucinda Grey's eyes, "you will never
convince Miss Grey that Halifax is a tolerable substi-
tute for York. As for me, I realize that I'm a dull dog,
and there's an end of the matter."

"Dull?" exclaimed Caroline, jumping to her feet, her
face indignant. "I should just like to hear anyone say
so to me, that's all!"

"There, my love, Will was jesting," said Mrs.
Arkwright, soothingly. "I am sure he knows that we do
not really think——"

"You have a staunch champion, sir," drawled Lucinda, eyeing Caroline mockingly.

The girl flushed, and subsided like a pricked bubble.
Mary darted an indignant glance at Miss Grey: she
could not like anyone who would unnecessarily wound
a child's feelings, and Caroline was at a particularly
vulnerable age.

"I have need of one," declared Arkwright. "Only
Caro will put up with me, isn't it so, my love?"

His deep tones gave a rich meaning to the casual en-
dearment. Caroline looked up, her eyes shining with
renewed confidence.

Mary began to wonder if she had misjudged her employer; he certainly seemed to show a more human side
within the family circle. Or was it Miss Grey's presence
which influenced him?

She did not have long to ponder the matter, for at
that moment Nellie appeared to say her master was
wanted.

"Who is it?" asked Artwright, frowning.

"Some o' t' lads from t' mill," answered Nellie, awkwardly.

"The mill, do you say?" He came quickly to his feet. "Nothing wrong, is there?"

"Nay, don't tak' on—it's nowt like that," said Nellie, hastening to reassure him. "They just want a word wi' thee, that's all."

"Indeed." He sat down again, his face stiff. "Tell them I shall be there as usual in the morning. Anything they may have to say will keep until then—I am occupied at present."

He nodded in dismissal, but she still lingered.

"I've told 'em so, already, but they'll not tak' no for an answer. Young John Booth's with them, and he insists——"

This time, Arkwright stood up so abruptly that he nearly knocked his chair over.

"Insists? John Booth, eh? We'll see about that."

He strode purposefully from the room.

Mary looked after him, a wave of apprehension sweeping over her. She had realized last night how little chance the proposed deputation had of succeeding in its object; but it could scarcely have picked a worse time for calling on Arkwright than when he was enjoying the company of a fascinating visitor. She gripped her hands tightly together in her lap, and could take no further part in the conversation which was going on around her.

Meanwhile, William Arkwright found the deputation awaiting him in the hall, where Nellie had marshalled them, after a great scolding and enforced wiping of boots. All but John Booth looked hangdog, and even he was plainly ill at ease.

Arkwright swept them with a contemptuous glance and wasted no words.

"Well, what is the meaning of this intrusion?"

For a moment, it looked as though he was to receive no answer and then John Booth spoke.

"We are sorry to interrupt your day of rest," he began, in a propitiatory tone. "But we have something to ask which cannot w-wait for—for—a more suitable t-time." His stutter started as he saw the frown deepen on Arkwright's brow, but he stuck to his guns. "Yesterday, you turned Sam Hartley off—a man who's served you f-faithfully for—for—many years, and who has a f-family of young children to—to—support——"

Arkwright cut him short ruthlessly.

"May I ask how this concerns you, Booth?"

It was Jack Hartley who answered that. "Nay, Maister, 't' were our notion to ask t' lad to speak for us. 'E didn't want to do it, neither—it's only goodness of heart on 'is part."

"He would do better to cultivate goodness of judgment," replied Arkwright, dryly. "And that's true of all of you. Take your grumbles to Nick Bradley—he'll know how to answer them. There is no shortage of labour hearabouts, let me remind you." He gestured towards the door. "That's all. I don't want to see you here again. The mill is one place—my house is quite another. Is that understood?"

He looked round grimly. For a moment, the men were overawed into silence. Again John Booth spoke up for them, his face pale, but determined.

"No." His mouth worked. "No. Mr. Arkwright, it's not all—Bradley is under y-your orders—he can do nothing in this. It is your responsibility—yours. Where else——" he struggled painfully for the words— "where else can they go to get their wrongs redressed——"

"I'll hear no more of this." Arkwright strode to the door, and flung it wide. "Do you think to question what I see fit to do in my own mill? That sounds like Luddite opinions to me, and I warn you once and for all that I'll make war to the death on all Luddites." He pointed towards the open door. "Any man who is not outside this house within the next minute, will find that he, too, is without work tomorrow."

One or two of them muttered mutinously at this, but there was nothing to be done: there were wives and families at home to be thought of. They began to slink out one by one, avoiding their employer's scornful eye. Eventually they all stood outside the house, a forlorn little group shivering in the cold wind which swept across the drive.

Only John still remained in the hall, his face work-

ing with emotion, but his attitude one of defiance.
Arkwright turned on him.

"Well, Booth. Do you go of your own accord, or do
I put you out? The choice is yours!"

John glanced wretchedly from Arkwright's stern
countenance to the dejected faces of the group outside.
Jack Hartley raised his head, his eyes meeting John's
in a desperate appeal. Courageously, the boy braced
himself to answer it.

"No, sir." His voice took on the note of hysteria
which it often held in times of crisis. Sitting in the parlour, her hands gripped tightly together, Mary could
hear every word that followed. "No—listen to me——"

"NO?" repeated Arkwright, his teeth coming together with a snap. "Then by God, I'll throw you out
neck and crop, puppy!"

He advanced upon John menacingly; the boy retreated a little, words spilling incoherently from his
twitching mouth.

"You must listen t-to me—s-sir—Sam Hartley—he
c-can't find another j-job in—in these p-parts—he—
he'll s-starve—his f-family——"

But Arkwright seized him by the scruff of the neck,
and began to propel him towards the open door.

"Stop!"

The mill-owner halted in surprise, and turned his
head. Mary Lister was standing in the hall, the parlour
door closed firmly behind her. She came forward
quickly.

"What is happening, Mr. Arkwright? My cousin—
why are you treating him in this way?"

"If you must know, ma'am," he replied grimly, "I'm
teaching him to mind his own business. Kindly leave
me to finish the lesson."

She faced him defiantly though her lips were trembling a little. "I have no intention of going," she said,
as firmly as she was able. "Whatever John has done,
surely it can all be settled in a civilized manner?"

"In a——" he stopped, astonishment momentarily
robbing him of words.

"I wonder, ma'am," he continued, menacingly, "if

you can have sufficiently considered the possible consequences of answering me in that fashion?"

He released John, and shut the front door with a
slam. He had no desire of an audience to this scene.
When he turned to face Mary again, he saw that her
face was pale, though she held her head high.

"All I can consider, Mr. Arkwright," she replied, in
a low voice, "is that my cousin is being handled
roughly. I cannot stand by and see it—how can you
expect that I should?"

He grunted, frowning heavily. "Your cousin is a
young fool, and like to land himself in serious trouble
if he continues in the way he's going at present. If
you've any real regard for his welfare, Miss Lister,
you'd do well to dissuade him from embroiling himself
in affairs that are no concern of his. Mark that well,
both of you, for I shan't give him another chance."

He turned on his heel, and left them standing there
in the hall.

8

The Stigma of Trade

LONG AFTERWARDS, MARY was to look back on those
early weeks of March as the calm before the breaking
of a storm. At the time, she could only feel thankful
that her life had settled into a more normal, peaceable
pattern.

John did not mention the unsuccessful deputation
again, although she sensed his disappointment and
feeling of personal failure. Wisely, she refrained from
forcing his confidence about George Mellor's presence
in the churchyard that day: he would turn to her more
readily in need, if in the meantime she did not pester
him with unwelcome questions.

Mr. Arkwright likewise made no further reference to

the affair. He and Mary were seldom in the house at the same time; during the day he was greatly occupied over at the mill and it was usual for Mary to return to the Vicarage in the late afternoon.

There were occasions, however, when he would walk into the house unexpectedly; and on one of these, he went up to the schoolroom.

Mary and Caroline were sitting together by the fire, Caroline reading aloud from a book in her hand. She looked up as he entered the room, and threw aside the book with scant ceremony.

He frowned. "That's no way to treat a book, miss."

"I'm sorry, Will." She picked up the book again, inspecting it. "Still, no harm has been done, as you see."

"No thanks to you," he retorted, stretching out his hand. "Let me have it."

She gave him the volume, which he scrutinized for a moment before passing it back to her.

"Hm. Poetry, I see. What has become of that book which you were reading with the M—with Miss Mercer?"

She pulled a face. "Oh, you mean Mentoria, or the Young Ladies' Instructor? I don't know for certain, but I only hope the Mouse took it with her. It was the most dreary thing! Only think, Will, how you would like to read long conversations between two of the most stuck-up females you could ever imagine on such subjects as Politeness, or The Use of Grammar!"

"It's very necessary for you to have a knowledge of those subjects."

"Oh, yes, but Miss Lister has a much better way of teaching them to me! She does it without my knowing—at least——"

She paused, crestfallen, as they both began to laugh. For a moment, she eyed them resentfully before breaking into laughter herself.

"Oh, well, you know what I mean! We have cosy little chats about journeying through different counties, for instance; and I know that I am learning a good deal about the geography of England, but I don't mind that, for it's all so much fun!"

"Hm!" His expression sobered, and he glanced at

Mary in a way she could not interpret. "So Miss Lister has methods of her own, has she? Let us put them to the test. Suppose you read to me from where you left off when I arrived?"

Caroline picked up the book, and found her place. She waited until he had settled himself in a chair before she began to read. He stared thoughtfully into the fire, listening to the sweet tones of the immature voice.

> "And was Jerusalem builded here
> Among these dark Satanic mills?
>
> Bring me my bow of burning gold,
> Bring me my arrows of desire,
> Bring me my spear, O clouds, unfold!
> Bring me my chariot of fire.
>
> I will not cease from mental fight,
> Nor shall my sword sleep in my hand,
> Till we have built Jerusalem
> In England's green and pleasant land."

He stopped her with a gesture of his hand. "That will do. You read very well, child, but have you any notion what it means?"

"I think so." Caroline looked at her governess for confidence; Mary gave a slight nod of encouragement. "I think it means that the poet wants to make a beautiful place of England, just as it was meant to be." She paused, frowning a little in concentration. "But I don't think he means only the look of the countryside, somehow——" She paused, searching for words. "He means people's thoughts—and—and aspirations, too——"

He nodded. "I dare say you're right. I'm not a poetical man, myself. Run along to your Mama for a while, Caro. I wish to speak to Miss Lister."

She hesitated. "You're not—vexed, Will?"

He gave her a direct glance. "I shall be, if you don't do what you are told. Off with you, now."

She obeyed, with a backward glance at Mary.

"What do you make of her?" he asked, when the door had shut.

"She's an excellent pupil," replied Mary, warmly. "Lively, original and intelligent. Her only fault is a tendency to impetuosity—sometimes it leads her into careless mistakes. But that is rare," she added, hastily.

"Mm." He tapped his fingers on the small table which stood close to his chair. "These methods of yours—they are somewhat unusual, I think. Where did you learn them?"

Mary considered for a moment before replying. "At home, I believe, with my own brothers and sisters. I found they were eager to learn, if only I could arouse their interest; and the simplest method was to weave all the facts into some kind of story that they could understand."

"Instruction without tears," he said, with a sardonic smile. "But I think you'll agree, Miss Lister, that a child's character must be trained, as well as its mind. If everything is to be made so pleasant, how will a child learn to face the oftentimes harsh realities of life? My chief concern for Caroline is that she shall become the kind of female who will one day make a good, dutiful wife."

"I cannot believe that pleasant instruction will prevent this," replied Mary, smiling. "She has a loving heart, and that will be her surest guide to her duty."

"Not at all." His tone was brusque. "Duty and love have little to do with one another. I should know that." He paused, staring into the fire. "Eight years ago, I did my duty by choosing to come here, and run my father's mill. Had I consulted my feelings in the matter, I should have remained in the Army."

"But it was affection for your family that dictated your choice," protested Mary.

He shook his head. "No. I scarcely knew my stepmother and Caroline. I suppose that sounds odd to you, but I had been away for so long—first at school, then with my regiment in various counties. My family were almost strangers to me."

"Whatever you felt once, you would not go back

now," said Mary, gently. "I have noticed—I could scarcely fail to do so—how fond you are of Caroline."

He laughed shortly. "Yes, love is a kind of blackmail, isn't it? But, in any case, there is no going back—that's one of life's little tricks, Miss Lister. One can't have yesterday——"

He broke off, brooding. She was silent, realizing that he was mentally reviewing the past, and had almost forgotten her presence.

"I wouldn't go back, if I could." The quiet words were tinged with bitterness. "I see now that I would always have remained something of an outsider. Oh, yes, I was popular enough—but there were the vague hints, the small but significant occurrences—the kind of thing that crops up when the Greys are here. At present, I can be useful in that quarter, therefore I'm being tolerated; but I've been warned not to get above myself." The bitterness was sharper now, so that the silent governess wondered how deep a hurt it revealed. "It was the same in the past—at school. Except that schoolboys don't favour vague hints. But I was like Caroline in those days, ready to trust, to laugh, and to forget injuries. And I was young, of course—young enough to believe that a man could be accepted for himself, regardless of his parentage."

Mary was startled into speech. "Parentage? But surely——"

He gave a short, mirthless laugh. He seemed to have forgotten that he was talking to one of his employees, a female to whom he paid a pittance of twenty pounds a year.

"Ay, parentage. Oh, nothing shocking, I assure you—at least, not to our way of thinking. But to gentlefolk, what can be more of a stigma than any connection with trade?"

A quick vision flashed across her mind's eye of the schoolboy that he had once been, with Caroline's dark curls and laughing face, and the bright eyes that looked eagerly out on the world. She heard in fancy the taunts he had suffered until he had learnt to check his homely Northern accent and avoid all mention of his father's mill. He might have suffered greatly, that boy, under the subtle tortures that schoolboys know only too well how to inflict on each other. Was this dark visaged, grim man who stood before her now the natural outcome of all that had gone before?

He rose abruptly, and began to pace the room in a way she was coming to recognize. It was as though he tried to keep pace with his thronging, urgent thoughts.

"One day they'll have to accept us," he said, his eyes kindling. "This is no longer a country given over solely to agriculture: and the possession of land which has been handed down from generations back will—in time—count for less than it has done in the past. The manufactories are fast becoming the country's life-blood, and we—the men who manage them—must eventually achieve social recognition."

He broke off, pausing in his stride: his eyes held a far-off look.

"What matters is that I should make a success of the mill," he muttered. "I cannot—must not—fail. Nothing must stand in the way——"

She understood. The schoolboy had given place to the man, but still William Arkwright strove to prove himself. She turned her head away, ashamed to have penetrated so far into his hidden consciousness, a deep compassion stirring within her.

Suddenly he turned, fixing her with a look of full awareness and slight dismay.

"Why the devil am I talking to you like this? You must think me mad."

She shook her head. "Not mad—lonely, perhaps?"

"Lonely, indeed. There has been no one——"

He broke off, and gave a short bitter laugh. When he spoke again, his voice had changed.

"I see you're a dangerous woman, Miss Lister—unwittingly, you lead people on to confide in you. I shall have to be on my guard."

Before she could answer, he strode from the room.

Throughout the rest of the day, Mary was unable to shake off the effect of this extraordinary conversation. She found herself returning to it again and again in the intervals between her lessons with Caroline. It was almost a relief to be able to ponder over it at leisure during the solitude of her short walk through the gathering dusk.

Arrived at the Vicarage, she removed her outdoor clothes and went in search of the housekeeper. A fragrant smell of baking led her to the kitchen. Mrs. Duckworth, sleeves rolled up to her rounded elbows, was just placing a large pie on a shelf in the oven, which shone like polished ebony. A diminutive urchin was standing meekly beside the white-scrubbed table, his whole being in his round eyes as he stared hungrily at the trays of pies and tarts which had been set out to cool.

Mrs. Duckworth finished her task, shut the oven door, and turned to greet Mary. Then she took a fair-sized meat pie from one of the trays, put it on a plate, and set it before the boy.

"There, lad! Get outside o' that."

He gabbled his thanks, seizing the pie in both hands and cramming it into his mouth as though the very process of eating took too long for the demands of his ravening appetite. But after a moment, he forced his hands to set it down again on the plate, while he groped for something in his pocket.

"What's up?" queried the housekeeper. "Bain't it to tha liking?"

He shook his tousled head vigorously, and produced a very dirty red kerchief.

"It's champion!" he replied, earnestly. "Reight champion, thank 'ee, ma'am! But——" he hesitated— "there's t' others. Reckon I've had my share."

She put out a plump, capable hand just in time to prevent him from wrapping the remainder of the pie in his handkerchief.

"Nay, lad! There's no occasion for that. Eat up, do. I've these for t' rest of t' family."

She indicated the contents of one large tray.

His eyes goggled, but his mouth was too full of pie for speech to be possible. Mary looked inquiringly at the housekeeper.

"It's Sam Hartley's eldest lad," explained Mrs. Duckworth. "Works at a mill over in Huddersfield—he's just got back from work. I asked him to call in on his way home, for Sam's that independent, I daren't put my nose in t' cottage with any food. T' lad will find a way to sneak it in, somehow, without his father finding out. But them poor brats are clemmed, leave alone Bess, who'll be brought to bed wi' another any day, now. Sam can get nowt, though he's tramped all over, asking for work. He's been out a fortnight, now, think on, Miss Mary. Things are bad there—very bad."

She shook her head, and began to parcel up the food for the boy. Mary studied him; he was not an attractive child, but she did not notice this. What she did see was the pallor of his face, accentuated by the effect of a pair of large eyes which were dark-ringed with weariness; and the frail body to which too little nourishment was offered in return for too much effort.

"How old is he?" she asked, unsteadily.

"Eleven, I think," replied Mrs. Duckworth, expertly tying her parcel. "He don't earn much, of course, but it's all they've got coming in."

"But—it's six miles to Huddersfield," said Mary. "How does he get there—does he go every day?"

"Shanks' mare, most often." The housekeeper saw that the last crumb was just being swallowed, and filled a mug to the brim with milk. She placed it before the boy, who drank eagerly. "Happen he might get taken up, now and then, if t' waggons are on t' road."

Mary swallowed, and blinked her eyes. "He needs boots," she said, in a strained voice. "I think—keep him here a moment longer, will you?"

She almost ran from the kitchen to her bedroom. Once there, she leaned against the door for a moment, fighting back the tears. She had thought she knew poverty. There was little to spare in her own home, and her uncle's scanty living had to be eked out by John's earnings at a saddler's. But poverty such as this, when the few shillings earned by a frail, weary child of eleven years old must serve to keep a whole family— this was something outside her personal experience.

After a moment, she pulled herself together, and went to a drawer in the big chest by the window. Opening a box, she took from it the remainder of the scanty hoard of money she had brought with her when she came to Liversedge. Her salary was due in a few day's time; she could manage until then.

She went back into the kitchen. The boy was waiting on a stool by the fire, his pinched cheeks for once aglow with warmth and repletion.

"What's your name?" she asked him.

He bobbed his head. "Tom, ma'am, please, ma'am."

"Well, Tom, I want you to do as I say. Take this ——" She handed him the money—"give some of it to your Mama, and with the rest buy yourself a pair of boots." She saw a look of doubt on the child's face, and pressed home her instruction. "You must have boots, Tom, for just now you are the family's wage-earner. You have that long walk to make every day, while the others may stay at home, you know. They are depending on you, so you must do everything to keep yourself well and strong."

He shook his head, and muttered words to the effect that his father would not like it, and would very likely leather him if ever it came to light.

Mary looked to Mrs. Duckworth for guidance, not caring to direct a child to deceive his own father.

"You do as t' lady says," insisted the housekeeper, firmly. "If tha father finds out, tell him as I told thee to do it, and threatened thee what *I'd* do, else. Sam knows all reight," she continued, turning to Mary, "that I don't stand no nonsense from any on 'em, child or man, it makes no odds."

She signalled to the boy to get down from the stool, and handed him the parcel.

"But if tha's got thy head screwed on t' reight road," she adjured, in parting, "tha'lt not let him see owt to make him vexed. Off tha goes, now."

9

Arkwright Makes a Concession

A FEW DAYS later, Mary was roused from sleep by the housekeeper at an unseasonable hour of the morning.

"I'm sorry, Miss Mary," she said, hurriedly, "but you'll need to get the breakfast this morning for yourself and Master John. Your uncle's been summoned to Sam Hartley's place—t' new baby's arrived, and like to die, and they want t' poor mite baptized before it goes. Bess Hartley's mortal bad, too, they say, and Sam's carrying on like one demented, cursing Arkwright and swearing vengeance, and upsetting poor Bess and t' little ones. They asked for me to go with t' Reverend, for they know as I stand no nonsense; happen Sam might listen to me, and calm down a bit."

Mary sat upright in bed, fully awake at this news. "Do you suppose I could do anything—or my cousin?"

Mrs. Duckworth shook her head. "Nay, lass. You've to go to your lessons presently; and as for Master John, t' least said to him, t' best, I'm thinking. You know what he is, and Sam needs firm handling, not sympathy, just now, by all accounts."

She quickly explained what was needed in the kitchen, then hurried from the room.

Mary rose and dressed, all the while turning over in her mind what she would say to John. Some explanation of the housekeeper's absence would be necessary, and she was almost tempted to invent an excuse. Knowing her cousin as she did, she was sure that he would take the bulk of the blame for this crisis on his own shoulders. He had felt his failure as leader of the deputation more deeply than he had ever allowed himself to show.

She cast about in her mind for a likely excuse only

to realize that eventually John must be told the truth.
To spare his feelings, she was prepared to lie to him
now; but when he discovered the truth later, it would
not be any less painful, and she would have forfeited
his confidence for nothing. She shrank from the unpleasant duty before her, but there seemed no escaping
it.

It proved as unpleasant as she had feared. After a
torrent of self-reproach John was for starting out at
once to the Hartleys' cottage. By then, he was in such
a highly emotional state that Mary dreaded the outcome if he and Sam should meet. She calmed him by
degrees, pointing out that his father and Mrs. Duckworth were already at the cottage, and that it would
not help Sam's wife in her present state to have a
crowd of people gathered round her. After a time, he
saw the sound sense of this, and agreed to defer his
visit until later in the day. It proved impossible, however, to persuade him to eat any breakfast.

"It would choke me, Mary! How can I eat, when I
kn-know that S-Sam's family have lately been l-living
on p-pigswill?"

"You don't mean that?" she asked, shocked.

He nodded, unable to answer for a moment.

"But surely the neighbours——" began Mary.

"They're almost as poor—and, anyway, Sam won't
take charity. Folks have had to find ways of smuggling
food into the house without his knowlege—but you
know that already. He's almost come to blows with his
own brother, Jack, on that score. He never forgets that
the croppers are skilled workers—he's got his pride,
poor chap, even if it's all he *has* got."

Mary was reluctant to leave him in this frame of
mind, but it was time for her to be setting out for the
Arkwrights' house. She impressed upon him again the
folly of going to Sam's at the present time, and believed that she had succeeded.

It was in a sombre mood that she began her daily
walk to her work. At any other time, she would have
taken pleasure in the first day of sunshine for many
weeks, in the burgeoning buds which tipped the
branches with green, and the birds' swift dartings from

tree to tree as they built their nests. Now all the stirrings of spring passed her by unnoticed. It was hard to
be so helpless to relieve another's misery: she could
think of nothing else.

She started violently when someone came up to her
and wished her good morning. She turned, and saw
that it was Mr. Arkwright. Her eyes opened a little
wider at sight of him. He was wearing the uniform of a
Captain of the Volunteers, a handsome affair with blue
facings and gold braid. She had not seen him dressed
in this way before; indeed, she had not realized that he
was a member of the Volunteer forces. It crossed her
mind that her mother would have called him a fine figure of a man. The red military coat set off his broad
shoulders to advantage, and gave an attractive devil-
may-care look to his usually stern face.

"No need to look so startled, Miss Lister," he said,
with a laugh. "I suppose you've seen a Militiaman before now?"

It was at once evident that he was in one of his
lighter moods. Mary tried to recall her wandering
thoughts.

"Oh—oh, yes," she stammered. "But I didn't
know—that is to say——"

"You didn't realize I was one of them?" he supplied,
swiftly.

She nodded.

"We've been out on exercises," he explained, swinging into stride beside her. "It's a splendid morning for
it, too."

He raised his head, and sniffed the crisp air appreci-
atively.

"I suppose so," admitted Mary, reluctantly.

He shot a quick glance at her, sensing that something was wrong. He made no comment, however,
changing the subject when next he spoke.

"You told me once you're from the country—do you
ride, ma'am?"

"I can," said Mary, brightening a little. "But I seldom do nowadays, for lack of a horse."

"Good." He smiled. "Young Caro rides very well,
and enjoys it. We must see what we can do to get you

both out together, though there's no prospect of finding you a mount from my own stable—if I can honour it with that title. It consists only of Caro's pony, Carrots, and my own horse—a bit long in the tooth, and never at best what one might call a prime stepper, I'm afraid. Still, a faithful servant, and worth his oats—as indeed, he has to be, for me to keep him. Everything—man, woman, child and horse—must earn its keep in the Arkwright household."

"Yes," said Mary, quietly. "I know."

He checked for an instant, and submitted her to a searching scrutiny.

"What do you know?" he asked. "Forgive me, Miss Lister, but is anything troubling you this morning?"

Afterwards, she could not tell why she should have given way to such humiliating weakness. Her eyes filled suddenly with tears; as she turned her face towards him, one quivered for a second on her long lashes, then fell onto her cheek.

He took her arm, and bent his head to look more closely into her face, which she quickly tried to turn away from him.

"What is it, lass?" Unconsciously, he used the familiar Yorkshire word, his tone as gentle as she was used to hearing it when he addressed Caroline. "Something's amiss—tell me."

She shook her head, unable to speak without breaking down.

"You've had bad news from home," he suggested, gently clasping her other arm and turning her round so that she was obliged to face him. "If there's anything I can do——"

She murmured something inarticulate, of which all he could distinguish was the word "No."

"Not from home?" She shook her head. "Then it's something to do with your uncle—or that cousin of yours?"

"No—not really——"

"Not?" He frowned, momentarily at a loss. Then his face cleared.

"It must be something at the house, then—my household, I mean."

He paused, and examined her face again. It was wet with tears; he thought how gentle and helpless she looked, like a frightened, small child, or a fledgling with quivering wings. He felt the stirrings of a protective instinct within himself. She was too young to be facing the world along—too young, and too attractive. It flashed across his mind that he himself had done nothing to make things any easier for her.

"Look here," he said, all at once becoming gruff with embarrassment. "If any of this is my fault——" he broke off for a moment—"Perhaps I'm not quite such a bear as I appear to be," he resumed. "My growl's worse than my bite. Only tell me, and we'll set it right, there's a good girl."

By this time, Mary was beginning to get a grip on her runaway feelings. She groped for a handkerchief, found it, and gently disengaged herself from his light clasp. She dried her eyes, blew her nose prosaically and stowed away the handkerchief. Then she faced him, her brown eyes looking calmly into his, which were so much darker as to be almost black.

"Forgive me, sir—I can't think why I should have given way to such foolish weakness."

"But there must have been a reason for all that," he insisted. "Won't you tell me what it is?"

"It would do no good," she replied sadly.

"How do you know?" he countered. "I suppose I am right in thinking that it is something that concerns my household—myself, perhaps?"

She nodded slowly. "In a way, yes."

"Then tell me," he urged.

She shook her head. "You would not want to know. It might even——"

"Might even—what?" He placed his hands upon her elbows again, and looked earnestly into her face. "Are you afraid of me, lass?" he asked gently. "You needn't be, you know—I wouldn't hurt you for the world."

Again their eyes met, and this time it was Mary who felt a faint stirring of some indefinable emotion. She pushed it quickly away, her mind too taken up with thoughts of Sam Hartley's predicament and her cousin's sense of guilt. Should she speak? Was it pos-

sible that in his new, gentler mood, Mr. Arkwright
might be worked upon to give Sam back his place in
the mill? Could she succeed where John had failed,
and bring comfort both to Hartley's family and her
cousin? She made up her mind in an instant.

"I will tell you," she said, trying to keep the nervousness out of her voice. "In a way, it does concern
you, though you have not done *me* any injury. It—it's
about Sam."

"Sam?" He repeated the name, puzzled.

"I mean Sam Hartley," she explained.

She saw a change come over his face. It tightened a
little, and he relaxed his hold on her arms.

"What have you to do with the labouring folk?" he
asked, abruptly.

"It's not that," she answered, and quickly told him
the story, stumbling a little here and there as she noticed how his expression gradually hardened.

When she came to the end, he was silent for a moment.

"We'd best walk on," he said shortly. "You'll get
cold, lingering here."

They stepped out together in silence, Mary's feelings
far from easy. She had hoped to influence him, but
now his mood had changed completely. Perhaps she
had done harm rather than good.

"Your cousin is an emotional young man," he said,
at last. "You mustn't allow him to upset you too
much."

"But it's not only that!" exclaimed Mary, stung to
protest by this cold comment. "Of course, I do not like
to see John distressed, but it was not the thought of his
sufferings which—which——" She faltered, and
stopped.

"Which made you cry," he interrupted promptly. "I
recollect now what I was saying that must have set you
off—I was talking of my horse being a faithful servant.
That is right, isn't it?"

She nodded, eyeing him warily but saying nothing.

"Well, Miss Lister," he continued, "Sam Hartley was
not a faithful servant, and so I got rid of him."

She turned to him impetuously. "What did he do

wrong, Mr. Arkwright? I have never heard of anything."

"Perhaps you may not always be so well-informed as
you seem to imagine," he said dryly. "I can think of
no reason why I should account to you, ma'am, for my
actions; but for once you may as well know the facts
from an authoritative source. Sam Hartley's a trouble-
maker, and a suspected Luddite. Even you and your
philanthropic cousin cannot expect me to employ a
Luddite in my mill. You surely cannot have forgotten
so soon what they are capable of."

She stared at him, and gave a quick shiver. "But are
you sure? John didn't seem to think——"

"I can't help but feel," he said, with a sneer, "that
my affairs would benefit considerably if they received
less attention from your young fool of a cousin. You
must really allow me, ma'am, to conduct my business
in my own way."

"There could be a mistake——" she faltered, un-
willing to relinquish her point, yet not daring to say too
much, for fear of angering him.

By now, they had reached the gates of the house: he
opened them a little way, and guided her through with
a firm hand placed beneath her elbow. He did not
speak again until he had closed the gates behind them,
and they were walking up the drive. She stole a sideways glance at him, and her spirits sank as she saw his
hard, inexorable expression.

"Possibly—possibly not. It's a risk I can't afford to
take, with things as they are in the West Riding at
present. There have been other matters in connection
with Sam—I'd have sent him packing long ago, if it
hadn't been for his brother, Jack, who's a good workman and a keen member of the Volunteers, into the
bargain. No, he's brought this on himself, and must
take the consequences."

They had reached the steps leading up to the front
door. He paused before mounting them, and looked
searchingly into her face.

"Well, mustn't he? What do you say?"

She shook her head, close to tears again.

"For God's sake," he said angrily, "take that look

off your face! Why the devil should I account to you
for my actions—tell me that?" Still she said nothing.
"I'm fighting a rearguard action here," he continued
bitterly. "If I lose, I'm done for—my livelihood's gone,
and that of my dependents. But the irony of it is that,
even if I win, it will be a hollow victory. I must forfeit
the good opinion of my workmen, and of people like
your cousin and yourself."

He waited for a moment, as though expecting an answer. When she remained silent, he turned away and
began to mount the steps. He raised the knocker, and
beat a tattoo that brought Nellie scampering to the
door.

"Very well," he said, before she had time to open it.
"Very well, Miss Lister, confound you! I'll see what
can be done for his family. I'll send Nick Bradley
round there later on. Now are you satisfied?"

10

Two Women

IT WAS SOME hours later that William Arkwright set
out for Halifax. He had important business with his
banker, business on which the whole future of the
Arkwright mill could well depend. In such circumstances, it might have been expected that his mind
would be occupied solely with the coming interview; in
point of fact, he did not give it more than a passing
thought. He was too busy trying to obliterate a mental
picture of a tearful pair of brown eyes. Damn the female, why did she have to concern herself with the
troubles of the labouring folk? Had she not worries
enough of her own—a fatherless girl, the eldest child
of a large family, with her living to earn? She would
get her desserts, he thought grimly, if she found herself
with an additional problem—that of looking for an-

other post. She seemed to forget that he had the power at any time to send her packing, or she would not defy him as she sometimes did. Undoubtedly these Booths were of the stuff of the Martyrs; though thank goodness Mary Lister was much more controlled than her young fool of a cousin. Indeed, her self-control at times was admirable, he decided, thinking back to the night when she had first arrived in Liversedge. How many women would have survived that ordeal without either falling into a deep swoon, or being seized by a violent fit of hysterics? But she had been calm, though pale and dark-eyed, and commendably silent on the subject of her personal sufferings. He reflected that it was only when the interests of others were at stake that she took fire, and leapt to their defence. He smiled, his eyes softening. She barely came up to his shoulder, and he could have lifted her from the ground easily with only one arm; but she had as stout a heart as any man who had ever served alongside him. In spite of that, she was completely feminine. It might be agreeable, he thought, to try out his theory of being able to lift her with one arm . . .

He pulled unexpectedly on the rein, causing his horse to swerve suddenly. With a muttered oath, he checked the animal, and turned his thoughts to more practical matters for the remainder of the journey.

The interview with his banker proved successful, and it was in a decidedly optimistic mood that he made his way to Colonel's Grey's lodging on the outskirts of the town. He was shown into the parlour, where the Colonel met him with a grave face.

"More incidents, Arkwright," he said. "They've broken into a mill at Rawdon, and smashed ten shearing frames. There's worse news from a man named Foster, at Horbury. You'll mind that a while back the magistrate there urged owners to get rid of their machinery, for fear of attack?" Arkwright nodded. "Well, it seems this man Foster had some spirit to him, and ignored the advice. He received one of the Luddite warning letters soon afterwards—you know the kind of thing?— signed by General Snipshears. He ignored that, too, except for bringing it to me, and setting his four sons to sleep nightly in his mill as a guard." He broke off, and shook his head. "It didn't suffice. The Ludds attacked in force, overpowered the four men, tied them to their beds and proceeded to wreck the place from end to end—frames, shears, benches, everything. There's not a whole window left in the mill. That was two days ago, and since then I've had several of the other manufacturers roundabout pestering me for troops to guard their property. The fact is, I can't do it, Arkwright, as you very well know—between you and me, I'm pretty well at a stand in this business, for lack of men."

"It's bad," agreed his visitor. "But there's always the Militia."

Colonel Grey shook his head. "You're not going to pretend that you think them the equals of the Regular Army? Besides, often as not they're involved with these people—relatives or friends of theirs."

"I know the difficulties, of course, sir. But the manufacturers themselves must take a firmer stand." He paused for a moment, then continued. "I suppose it's no use, then, bringing you my request?"

The Colonel raised his eyebrows. "Never tell me that now you're demanding troops to guard your place! I must say, I thought better of you, Arkwright."

"Not exactly." Arkwright's mouth set in a grim line. "I fancy if need be I shall make do with a small band of picked men from among the Volunteers in my own command. No, what I am after is to borrow two or three of your men just for a few hours one night in order to escort my new machines from the manufactory in Huddersfield to my own premises. I won't trust any local men, after what happened before."

Colonel Grey chuckled. "So you're not put off by the fate of your previous consignment? B'Gad, Arkwright, I like your spirit! It's a thousand pities you ever left the Service—we could do with men like you in the Peninsula at present."

A shadow crossed the mill-owner's face. "Believe me, sir, I myself had rather be there than here—but my duty lies here, if my family is not to suffer." He broke off, and shrugged—"However, I don't mean to burden you with my personal affairs. Can you lend me the men, Colonel?"

The older man considered for a moment. "For that length of time, yes. How many d'you want? Armed, I suppose?"

"A dozen should suffice," replied Arkwright. "Yes, armed—and prepared to shoot almost on sight. I haven't forgotten the last time the Ludds killed one of my men."

"Queer we never found out any more about that," mused the Colonel. "In spite of the notices which were posted everywhere proclaiming fifty pounds reward for information."

"It doesn't surprise me, sir. Someone knows something, of course, but they keep their mouths shut through either loyalty or fear."

"A bit of both, I dare say," said the Colonel. "This Oath the Luddites take is a damned fearsome thing. We've had the gist of it from a spy who was working in Nottingham at one time. He's dead now."

Arkwright looked a question; Colonel Grey nodded.

"Yes—their work, of course. Still, he was useful—while he lasted."

"I should never be surprised to learn that the same fate had overtaken the spy who's in my own mill. Whether anyone yet suspects what he is, I can't say; but he's caused some trouble already."

"Trouble?"

"Nothing I can't handle," replied Arkwright, firmly, and rose to leave. "I can count on your men, then? I'll let you have full details tomorrow."

As he was leaving the house, he met Miss Grey and her companion in the hall. Lucinda was wearing a cherry coloured travelling dress trimmed with white fur; she stood out in cheerful contrast to the sombre furnishings which surrounded her.

"Well, who could have guessed," she greeted him, with an arch smile, "that you would have taken the trouble to come in person to escort me to Liversedge?"

"Do you go to Liversedge, Miss Grey?"

She looked reproachful. "Surely you cannot have

forgotten that I promised to take luncheon with dearest Caroline on the first fine day?"

He looked out of the windows. "You call it a fine day, do you, ma'am?"

"Well, there is sun, and it is not quite so cold. What more do you want, sir? Or perhaps you do not wish me to come?"

Her blue eyes mocked him. He smiled slightly.

"On the contrary, I cannot imagine anything more delightful for my sister."

The last words were added after a scarcely perceptible pause. She pouted.

"Oh, that does not sound very convincing! Will you not like to have me there, too?"

"Lucinda, my dearest," interrupted her chaperone, all of a twitter. "Pray recollect——"

Miss Grey turned a cold look upon the plump lady. "Do not be so stupid, Cousin Lottie," she said, represssively. "That is, if you can help it."

Arkwright frowned a little. "We shall all be honoured," he said, bowing slightly. "May I ride with you? I have finished my business in Halifax."

She graciously gave permission. "Though I do not undertake," she concluded, "to keep the window down all the way so that we may converse."

"I wouldn't ask it," he replied, laughing, "otherwise you might contract the toothache, or some such malady."

It was her turn to frown. She did not care to be associated in any man's mind with aches and pains. She said no more until the carriage was at the door, and then she allowed him to help the plump Miss Foster and herself up into it, with an almost regal air of condescension.

As he mounted the horse which had been brought round for him, he reflected that Miss Grey could do with a sound smacking. It was a pity that, in spite of this, he should find her such an unsettling female.

He had ample time to develop this theme on the ride home. Having once briefly let down the window in order to speak to him, Lucinda decided that the air was too cold for Cousin Lottie, and hastily shut it again.

Arkwright was considerably amused by this remark. He was willing to hazard a fair sum that concern for others did not often govern Miss Grey's actions. The brief insight turned his thoughts for a moment towards that other female who had occupied them during his ride to Halifax. Each had her own attraction, he reflected, although in character they were very different. He was quite used to the Miss Greys of this world: he had met and enjoyed the company of a good many of them in his days as a young Army officer. They promised everything, and meant nothing. His sister's governness was the more dangerous of the two, for whatever she did was meant in earnest. He shrugged, smiled, and, catching a glimpse of Lucinda's perky bonnet through the window of the carriage, drew nearer. She turned her head, and rewarded him with a sunny smile.

They continued side by side in this way until Liversedge was reached, when Arkwright reined in to follow behind the carriage. When they came to the gates of the house, the coachman swung round into the drive, finishing the last few yards at a spanking pace.

They had almost reached the house, when without warning a figure stepped out from the thick laurels which bordered the drive, and stood right in the path of the oncoming horses.

The coachman shouted, swerving his horses violently and missing the pedestrian by inches. The ladies screamed in terror as the coach swayed perilously, remaining upright by a miracle. Arkwright, following close behind, was caught off his guard by the unexpected movement of the vehicle. He reined in sharply, his horse reared, and he was almost thrown. Jumping from the saddle, he spared only a moment to try and quieten the animal before leaving it to find its own way round the back of the house to the safety of its stable. Then he strode angrily towards the cause of the trouble.

It was a man. He stood there clutching a bundle wrapped in a tattered blanket, and he neither moved nor spoke as Arkwright approached him.

"Are you mad, fellow?" stormed Arkwright.

"Jumping out in front of us like that! Someone might
have been killed!"

The man spoke then. "Someone 'as been killed,
Maister Arkwright." He moved forward a few paces,
and in spite of his wild eyes and dishevelled state, the
mill-owner recognized Sam Hartley. "Ay, someone's
been killed, reight enough, an' 'tis thy doin', think
on—thine, I tell thee! Look—look'ere—look at thy
work, and feel proud on 't!"

He held out the bundle, and with shaking fingers began to uncover it.

Arkwright recoiled in horror, and cast a quick
glance behind him. The ladies had alighted from the
carriage, and were just coming over to see what was
the cause of the trouble. He shouted to them to stay
where they were.

"For God's sake, man, cover it up again!" he urged.
"The ladies——"

Sam laughed wildly. "Oh, ay, t' ladies mustn't set
eyes on a dead child," he mocked. "But my Bess could
watch it die, afore she went herself—tha reckons that's
a' reight, Maister bloody Arkwright? Two on 'em," he
went on, his voice rising hysterically. "Two on 'em—
mother and baby—an' both can be laid at thy door—
murderer!"

"Hold your noise!" Arkwright spoke sharply, knowing hysteria was close. He glanced behind him. Miss
Foster had obeyed his order, but Miss Grey was standing close at his elbow. His glance told her what he
thought of this action, but he had no words to waste on
her at that moment. He turned again to Sam.

"Go home, Sam," he said, quietly. He reached out,
and pulled the blanket back into place. "You're overwrought at present—small wonder. But this will do no
good, as you'll realize when you're calmer."

He plunged his hand into his breeches pocket, and
held it out towards the man. "Take this. It may help.
I'll send Nick Bradley round later to see what can be
done for you and your family. Go now."

Sam Hartley stared at the outstretched hand for a
moment, as though his eyes refused to focus. Then,
with a sudden violent movement, he thrust it away.

The gold piece Arkwright was clutching fell from his grasp, and rolled on the ground to land at Sam's feet.

"Brass!" Sam said, vehemently. "Tha reckons brass can buy owt, can mak' wrong reight, and give a mother back to her family, don't tha, Maister? Well, I'll tell thee what tha can do with tha brass—ay—and wi' t' whole stinking rotten———"

He broke off as the sound of pounding feet was heard close at hand: a moment later, John Booth burst suddenly upon the group.

Breathlessly, he turned to Sam. "For God's sake, Sam, come away at once!" He turned to Arkwright. "I hope I'm in time—he hasn't———"

His eyes travelled to Miss Grey.

Arkwright shook his head. "No harm's been done. Take him home, Booth. And try if you can to persuade him to use that"———he indicated with a glance the guinea lying at their feet—"to relieve his immediate necessity. Maybe he'll listen to you."

"I'd die sooner!" shouted Sam. "And mark my words, Maister Arkwright. I'll get even with thee for this day's work, see if I don't, tha bloody murderer!"

Before John could move to prevent it, he spat full in Arkwright's face.

Miss Grey looked with some curiosity at the mill-owner to see what he would do. In some odd way, she found herself almost enjoying this scene. If she judged her man aright, he would take a horsewhip to the workman who had just offered him such an indignity.

She was to be disappointed. Arkwright merely produced a handkerchief, and wiped his face. Then he nodded silently to John Booth to take the man away.

The fury born of Sam's anguish had now burned out, leaving him broken and dejected. John put an arm as gentle as a woman's about him, and led him unresisting away.

"Well!" exclaimed Lucinda. "What was all that about, pray?"

"A business matter," said Arkwright, tersely.

"Do you always conduct your business in such a dramatic style?" she persisted, refusing to be put off by his discouraging manner.

"Miss Grey, you may perhaps not have understood. That man had just lost his wife and newborn child. In such circumstances, a little drama is excusable, you will allow."

"Oh, yes, by all means."

"Shall we go in?" he said, moving to join Miss Foster, who was still standing beside the coach. "I am glad to observe that the incident has not affected you in any way."

If she noticed the irony in his tone, she gave no sign of it. "No, why should it affect me? And, I dare say, you know, that presently that man will realize that it is no very bad thing to have two less mouths to feed."

He looked at her as though seeing her for the very first time.

11

Caroline Is Missing

IT SEEMED TO Mary that at last she had achieved a good relationship with her employer. He had always been the one uncertain factor in the household; she had never been sure from day to day what kind of mood she would find him in, whether it would be politic for her to talk freely to him or to keep silent. But now, after each had betrayed to the other on different occasions some of the thoughts which were normally kept hidden from the world, surely future encounters would be on a more friendly, equable plane.

She was to be speedily disillusioned, and to discover that she had not yet seen the worst of William Arkwright's autocratic temper.

It began a few days after Sam Hartley buried his wife and child. Talk from the servants had drifted to Caroline's ears, and she had been asking questions of her mother and Mary which they had done their best to avoid. Both knew it was Arkwright's policy to try and keep Caroline away from any contact with his business affairs; whatever Mary may have thought of this, she was obliged to do what was expected.

Towards the middle of the morning, Mary left Caroline practising alone at her pianoforte in the parlour, while she herself sought the quiet of the schoolroom in order to prepare the next lesson. It was quite usual for her to do this; the sound of the pianoforte did not reach as far as the schoolroom, but she knew she could trust Caroline to spend the required time on her exercises.

At the end of the hour agreed upon, she returned to the parlour to find it empty. At first she thought nothing of this; Caroline's absence would be only temporary. She wandered over to the instrument, and inspected the music propped up on the stand.

It was then that she began to suspect that Caroline might have evaded her duties, and been absent for some time. The book was open at the first page which she had been told to practise; while the rest of the music which had been part of her morning's task was lying untouched on the top of the pianoforte, just as Mary herself had placed it.

She frowned. There might be a satisfactory explanation of all this, but she meant to hear some kind of explanation immediately. She went into the hall, called Nellie, and asked her if she knew anything.

Nell shook her head. "No, ma'am, only I haven't heard her playing for some time. Happen she's up in her room, bad lass, or out in t' garden. I'll send after her, and bring her to you directly."

Mary thanked her and sat down at the pianoforte to play until her errant pupil should arrive. No doubt Caroline's quick mind had thought of something which could not wait a moment to be done, and she had dashed off to execute her plan, not meaning to be more than a few minutes away from her appointed task.

It was quite a long time before Nellie returned, alone. She look worried.

"She 'bain't nowhere, not in t' house nor t' garden, ma'am. Where can she have got to?"

"I can't imagine," replied Mary, a worried frown creasing her brow. "She is not with Mrs. Arkwright, I suppose?"

Nell shook her head. "Mistress went visiting more'n two hours agone. Miss Caro was still with you, ma'am, in t' schoolroom, then."

"What about the mill? Perhaps she's walked over to see her brother."

"I don't reckon she'd do that, Miss Lister. She knows as Maister don't welcome her there, think on."

"No," said Mary, thoughtfully. "But there might have been something which seemed to her to be too urgent to wait until Mr. Arkwright returned home this evening. You know how impatient she is."

"I do an' all." Nell's grey head nodded emphatically. "But I don't reckon she'd go agin Maister Will for all that, ma'am."

"Perhaps not. All the same, I think I'd better walk over there, and make sure. If she appears in the meantime, will you send someone after me to let me know?"

The housekeeper promised, and Mary hurried upstairs to put on her pelisse and bonnet.

She had never before visited the mill. It lay in a hollow beside a pleasant stream, partly shielded from the view of the house by a thin belt of trees. When she reached the building, she stood for a moment on the paved forecourt, considering the massive wooden front door studded with huge iron nails. She doubted if anyone would hear if she knocked on such a door, and there did not appear to be any other means of attracting attention.

While she was hesitating, a man crossed the yard. He stopped on seeing her and approached. She recognized Nick Bradley.

He greeted her cordially, and asked if he could be of any help.

"I wondered if Miss Caroline had come here," said Mary. "She's missing from the house."

He shook his grey head. "Not as I know of, ma'am; but happen tha'll want to talk to Maister Will—he may know summat."

Mary's heart sank, but she nodded. "If you'll be

good enough to take me to him, I think it would be best."

As it happened, he was spared the trouble, for at that moment Arkwright himself came through the great door, a look of concentration on his face. It changed at sight of Mary.

"Miss Lister! What in thunder are you doing here?" Then, more sharply: "Is anything wrong?"

Mary told him, trying to sound less worried than she felt.

"What's this?" he interrupted, brusquely, before she had time to finish. "Caroline missing, you say? Missing? And pray what were you about, to let her get out of your sight, ma'am?"

She began to explain that it was usual for her to leave Caroline alone to practise at the pianoforte, but again he cut her short.

"We'll go into that later. Where had you looked for her, beside here?"

"Only around the house and garden," faltered Mary, taken aback by the severity of his tone. "I didn't quite know——"

"You should know, Miss Lister—it's your duty to know."

"She may have returned by now," said Mary. "She can't have gone far——"

"No?" he asked, fiercely, glaring at her. "But it's no use standing here—let's go back to the house. Nick——"

He turned to Bradley, and issued some instructions in a quick, terse voice. The man nodded, smiled briefly and sympathetically at Mary, and hurried away.

Arkwright strode back along the path at a pace which made it impossible for Mary to keep up with him. She arrived breathless at the house, to find him already in the kitchen, impatiently questioning the entire domestic staff.

They had nothing to tell him. Miss Caroline had been seen neither indoors nor out, since first thing that morning.

"You're a bunch of incompetent half-wits, and by God! if anything's happened to your young mistress, I'll—I'll flay you alive!" he threatened, grimly. "Right

—Ben, you go down to the village. Question everybody, look everywhere. If you miss anything, never think to come back here again. Harry, you go in the other direction—do the same. Molly——"

He issued rapid directions to all of them, his face tense with anxiety.

"Off you go!" he concluded, and turned to Mary, who alone was left.

"And now, ma'am, we'll go together. Nell's in the house, in case Caro returns; and I may need your womanly offices, if we find her." He stopped abruptly, torn by the thoughts these words raised. "Damn you, Miss Lister!" he finished, his eyes fierce. "If any harm's come to her——"

"But," stammered Mary, "I don't quite see, sir, what harm could come to her. She may simply have gone for a walk——"

"Fiddle! What you don't know, woman, is that Sam Hartley was outside this house a few days ago, swearing to take vengeance on me for what he considered to be the murder of his wife and child. He knows well enough—they all know—what I think of Caro. What better vengeance than——"

He choked on the words. She had never seen him so moved, and would not have believed it possible.

"Oh, no!" she exclaimed, shocked. "Surely no one could harm a child? Pray don't let your fears run away with you——"

"It's easy to see you've led a sheltered life, Miss Lister. A few more months here will soon change that. Come—we're going to Sam Hartley's cottage—but there's something I must get first."

He strode out of the kitchen. When he returned, he was carrying the coachman's whip. She stared at it in horrified fascination, realizing the use for which it was intended. She realized, too, the powerful forces which might be unleashed if William Arkwright should take one false step in dealing with Hartley. She thought of black George Mellor, and shuddered.

"Do you think you should—take—that?" she ventured to say.

"I may need it," he answered, grimly.

"But Caroline may not be there at all——"

"That I mean to discover. Come on."

He took her arm, and half dragged her from the kitchen.

They spoke no word as they made their way across the fields to the spot where Sam Hartley lived. She glanced once only into his face, and looked quickly away from the grim mask which she guessed was hiding extremes of hate and suffering.

Ten minutes sharp walking brought them to a small farmhouse situated not more than a few hundred yards from the group of dilapidated cottages of which Sam Hartley's was one. A dog barked at them as they passed, but they saw no one about in the yard.

Now that he was within sight of his objective, Arkwright's stride lengthened, so that Mary had great difficulty in keeping up with him. The ground was rough here, too; the tussocky grass concealed rabbit holes, and she was forced to tread with care, keeping her eyes firmly fixed on the ground.

Suddenly she let out a little cry, and pounced on an object which she had seen lying on the grass just in front of her.

Arkwright checked, and came to her side.

"What is it? What have you found?"

She turned the object over in her hand, then held it up for him to see. It was a blue woollen glove.

"It's Caroline's," she said, uneasily. "Mrs. Arkwright only finished making these for her a few days since——"

He nodded, and his face tightened. "She's here, then," he said. "I thought as much."

He began to run towards the cottages.

"But wait!" called Mary.

He halted for a moment, to allow her to catch up with him. Then he took her arm roughly.

"There's no time to lose, and I must have you with me, in case she—needs you. Come on, woman, you must hurry—God knows what's happening in there."
He jerked his head in the direction of the cottages.

"But surely she might have gone to the farm, since

we found her glove close by," argued Mary. "Hadn't we better make sure, first, before——"

"Why should she go to the farm, tell me that?"

"Why should she go to Sam Hartley's cottage, for that matter?" replied Mary, reasonably; although she felt more and more apprehensive as they covered the short distance that divided them from the cottages.

"Some trick, no doubt—we'll find out—so will he, by God!"

She could not argue any more, for she needed all her breath for the headlong race to cover the intervening distance. Arkwright's hand gripped her arm like a vice as he half-pulled, half-pushed her along.

As they reached the first cottage in the row, they heard the sound of someone chopping wood at the rear of the building.

"This is Hartley's place," muttered Arkwright, abruptly releasing Mary so that she almost fell forward on her face. "Now we'll see!"

He raised his fist, and beat a loud tattoo on the rickety door. A child's face appeared at the nearby window, to be joined presently by another and younger one. After a pause, the door opened.

A thin, pale girl of about nine years of age stood on the threshold. She shrank back at sight of Arkwright. He pushed her aside, and strode into the cottage, while Mary remained hesitating on the step, trying to regain her breath.

The door opened straight into the only downstairs room of the building, apart from a crazy wooden lean-to at the rear, which served as a primitive kind of scullery. Arkwright's fierce gaze travelled swiftly over the bare, yet clean, room with its few battered pieces of furniture, and its tiny fire smouldering in the spotless grate. A baby was crawling about the floor; it began to snivel, and the child who had admitted Arkwright picked it up, and held it close to her. The other children in the room all drew closer to this one, who was the eldest. They stood in a defensive little group, watching the newcomers with wary eyes that held no suggestion of interest or vitality.

"Is there a girl here?" asked Arkwright, impatiently.

They stared at him without answering.

"A girl—a young lady of fourteen—have you seen her?" he insisted, advancing on the group.

They shrank away from him, but still made no answer.

He muttered an oath under his breath, and ran his fingers through his hair. Then he turned to Mary.

"For God's sake see if you can get them to answer," he flung at her.

She advanced into the room, and smiled encouragingly at the children.

"Do you know who this gentleman is?" she asked, in a quiet voice.

The eldest girl considered him gravely, then nodded. "Maister Arkwright, from t' mill."

"And do you know his sister, Miss Caroline?" went on Mary, persuasively.

Again the girl nodded. "Ay. She's t' lass wi' t' pretty bonnets who stands next 'im, in t' church of a Sunday."

"That's right." Mary smiled approvingly. "Has she been here? Have you seen her today?"

The child's eyes opened wide. "Nay. What for should she come 'ere?"

"She must be here!" exploded Arkwright. "We found her glove, didn't we?"

"Yes, but——" began Mary.

"The child's lying," he said, fixing the little group with a fierce stare. "Here, you—what's-your-name—just tell me the truth, now, or it'll be the worse for you!"

He took the child by the arm. His grasp was not rough; but the girl, frightened and uncertain of the outcome, let out a shriek of terror. This started the others shrieking like a pack of demons let loose.

Arkwright turned in dismay to Mary; but before she could attempt to put matters right the door leading to the outhouse swung open, and a man charged into the room, a hatchet in his hand.

It was Sam Hartley. He took one look at the scene, then plunged forward with a bellow.

"Tak' tha dirty hands off my children, Maister

bloody Arkwright—tha's done enough damage to me an' mine, I reckon, an' now I'll settle t' score!"

He raised the hatchet, and flung himself on Arkwright.

A scream rose involuntarily to Mary's lips, but she did her best to stifle it. She must not add to the children's terror. She put her arms about them, and hastily shepherded them into a corner of the room, where they huddled together, shivering and crying. At the same time, a thunderous knocking sounded on the door, and voices clamoured for admittance.

She shot a frightened glance at the two men. They were swaying together in the middle of the room, Arkwright's fingers clamped tightly about Hartley's wrist in an effort to force him to drop the hatchet. With his free hand, the mill-owner was raining blows on the other man's body: he seemed to have the best of it, as far as she could judge.

She ran to the door and flung it open. There was a small crowd outside, composed chiefly of women and children from the surrounding cottages, who had come running when they heard the screams of the Hartley children. There were two men among them: they shouldered their way to the door, and leapt into the room as they saw what was happening there. Mary noticed with relief that one of them was Nick Bradley. She did not know the other, but he was reassuringly burly.

They wasted no words at that moment, but flung themselves on Sam Hartley, pinioning his arms behind him so that the hatchet fell with a clatter to the floor.

Arkwright stepped back, tossing his head to shake back a lock of dark hair which had fallen over his eyes. For a few moments, Sam Hartley struggled, shouting abuse at his captors; but he was no match for the two of them. He was forced to capitulate at last and stood helplessly in their grasp, too short of breath even for further abuse.

"What's to do, Maister?" asked Bradley, panting.

Arkwright turned to the open door. "We'll have this shut, by your leave, Hartley," he said. "I dare say you've no more fancy than I have to provide a raree show for the neighbours."

The assembled women and children were still waiting, agog with curiosity, on the doorstep. Much to their chagrin, Arkwright closed the door in their faces.

"That's better," he said. "Now"———his tone changed to one of menace—"where is my sister?"

Sam Hartley stared incredulously. "I don't know— nor care! What I'd like to know is what reight tha's got to come bustin' in my house, an' frightin' my young 'uns———"

"Wait a bit," interrupted Nick Bradley. "Tha's got it wrong, Maister—Miss Caro 'bain't 'ere. She's over at t' farm. She twisted 'er ankle in a rabbit 'ole, and managed to hobble there. Jem———" he glanced at his companion—"will tell thee that's reight. Eh, Jem?"

The farmer nodded. "It 'appened not long since. Missus took t' lass indoors, and set to bathin' her ankle, an' such like. I sent a lad up to t' mill with a message for thee, Maister Arkwright———"

Nick nodded. "Ay. He arrived not ten minutes after tha'd left t' mill wi' Miss Lister. I went over to t' house, sithee, thinkin' to find the pair o' ye there. Nell told me tha'd gone lookin' for t' lass, and I reckoned tha might head this way, so I followed. When I reached t' farm, Jem was just coming out. One o' his lasses 'ad been upstairs, and she'd gone to t' winder when she heard t' dog barkin', and seen thee passin' by wi' Miss Lister."

"T' silly wench didn't say nowt till tha'd gone reight past, Maister Arkwright," put in Jem Hobson. "Otherwise I'd ha' caught thee afore tha reached Sam's place."

"Better if tha had," muttered Bradley, looking askance at his master.

Arkwright's face betrayed nothing of what he felt. "You say Miss Caroline's hurt her ankle? But what was she doing down here, in the first place?"

The farmer shook his head. "She didn't say—leastways, if she did it was to t' missus, not me. Happen she came for a bit of a walk, like."

Arkwright shook his head. "No. I think not." He turned to Hartley again. "What do you know of all this?" he asked, suspiciously.

"Nowt," Hartley panted, still breathless from his recent exertion. "For all I care thee an' thine can roast in Hell—ay, and will, what's more, if tha gets thy desserts."

"You persist in saying that you know of no reason why my sister should come this way?"

"I do that. And now get out o' my house, Maister Arkwright, and tak' tha rotten wage-slave wi' thee. And yon wench——" indicating Mary with a gesture of his head—"I don't want t' likes o' her hangin' round my children."

"Watch your tongue!" warned Arkwright, imperiously.

"I'll say what I like in my own house," replied Sam, defiantly. "I got some reights, like young Booth's always tellin' us. And one o' them reights is," he went on, raising his voice, "to be shot o' company as I don't want, nor haven't invited, neither. So get out, t' lot o' ye."

Arkwright signalled to the others. "We're going, Hartley. But understand this—if I find later that you were in any way involved——"

"What canst do that's worse nor what tha's done already?" queried Hartley, bitterly. "I've nowt to fear from thee, Maister Arkwright—now."

12

The Dark Rider

"I'VE BEEN QUESTIONING Caroline," began Arkwright, abruptly, coming into the schoolroom where Mary was sitting alone. "It seems she'd heard some talk about the Hartleys, and was going there to take them money."

Mary nodded. "I'd already guessed as much. It would be like her."

He looked at her searchingly. "Have you any particular reason for coming to that conclusion?"

"No," she said, slowly. "Except that she had been asking a good many questions about Sam Hartley during the last few days."

"What kind of questions?"

"Oh, about his dismissal from the mill, and his family's circumstances—that kind of thing, you know."

He kept his eyes on her face, and she felt herself colouring under the keen scrutiny. "Knowing your own interest in that family, it did occur to me that you might have initiated these questions."

"How could you think that?" she asked indignantly. "I knew very well that you did not wish Caroline to concern herself with such matters."

"Am I to suppose that my wishes would weigh with you?" he countered, with a sneer.

"Certainly. I am paid to regard them."

"I am relieved to hear you say so, for I thought it had slipped your memory."

"What makes you say that?" She had started by feeling apprehensive, but now she was becoming indignant. She was prepared to be held responsible for Caroline's escapade, but not blamed for initiating it. "I am not conscious of ever having disregarded them."

"It is a part of your duty to keep a strict watch on your charge. Had you done this, today's incident would not have been possible. Can you suppose that you were acting in accordance with my wishes when you made a habit of leaving her entirely unsupervised for one hour in every day?"

"I'm not trying to evade my responsibility for what happened, sir. I could plead that it never occurred to me that Caroline might abuse——"

"It should have done," he interrupted. "What use is a guardian who does not foresee possible trouble?"

"It never seemed possible to me that Caroline should deceive me—I had judged her incapable of it."

"You are too trusting," he sneered. "This is not your first experience of children, I understand?"

"Mr. Arkwright," she said, with emphasis. "I know —we both know—that only something quite out of the ordinary would induce your sister to behave in this way. Her escapade was unpremeditated—she acted on the spur of the moment." She took a deep breath to fortify herself. "Am I then expected to regulate Caroline's routine to allow for the extraordinary events? If so, it must be an extremely rigid one."

"Do you presume to argue with me?"

"No," she replied, marvelling at her own temerity. "Merely to bring to your notice a point which may have escaped it."

"Upon my word, ma'am," he answered sharply, "I begin to wonder if you are fit to have charge of my sister at all! This defiance is not what I look for in one circumstanced as you are."

The hint was unmistakable, but some unruly spark in Mary prompted her to try her luck further.

"My circumstances are not of my making, sir. Perhaps it is scarcely generous in you to allude to them. Surely in justice I may defend myself?"

"You——" He advanced upon her angrily. She fell back a step, looking at him in alarm. For a moment they stood motionless, staring into each other's eyes.

"B'God!" he muttered, at last. "You don't know what you do, woman!"

She did not dare say any more. For a moment there was silence.

"Very well," he continued, in a more normal tone. "We will have a complete understanding, Miss Lister. First of all, you will see to it that your charge is never left alone during the hours that you are employed here. If for any reason you are unable to be present, she must be left in the care of some other responsible person. You see that I am classing you as a responsible person, in spite of everything." She darted an indignant look at him, but made no remark. "And secondly, I am going to give you a warning—it's the last you will hear from me. I've stood a good deal from your family of late, and I'm beginning to feel that my affairs will go on very well without them. Caroline is very fond of you, so I have promised this time to overlook your shortcomings." He paused, regarding her sternly. "I've been very patient, ma'am, and I'm not a patient man. Consider this well, before you venture to cross me again."

He stalked out, and Mary was left to consider the interview, and to marvel at herself. How could she have dared that temper? She realized how close she had come to being dismissed; yet, at the time, she had been unable to suppress her indignation. She had behaved quite differently from what she had intended. She had meant to ask his pardon for her dereliction of duty. But there was something about the man which roused personal feelings in her which overcame her natural prudence. She must be more on her guard in future.

She slept fitfully that night, the interview with Arkwright springing clearly to her mind each time she awoke. Just before dawn, she was beginning to settle more peacefully, when she was aroused by sounds from outside.

She sat up in bed, fear clutching at her with cold fingers. Was it the Luddites on the march again?

She listened for a moment. No: this was not the same sound that she had heard once before in the night. She could distinguish wheels and horses' hoofs; these were waggons going past, escorted by men on horseback.

She leapt out of bed, and to the window, pulling side the curtain. A clear moon floated high above the scudding clouds. It lit the scene, showing Mary a flash of red coats riding by, and the grey shape of a waggon. For a moment, a dark head was outlined sharply against the sky before its owner rode past. In that brief flash Mary recognized her employer.

She climbed back into bed again with cheeks that burned.

The next day, Caroline's ankle showed some signs of improvement, so that her routine needed little change. Both she and her governess felt disinclined to discuss the events of the previous day; they shared a slight depression of spirits.

It was with relief, therefore, that they joined Mrs.

Arkwright in the afternoon for tea in the parlour. Caroline's mother was invariably cheerful, and would soon present them with some trivial subjects about which they could chat comfortably. Sure enough, by the time the tea cups had been handed round, Caroline was smiling and Mary was feeling much more at ease.

This pleasant atmosphere was shattered abruptly by the unexpected entrance of the master of the house. At sight of him, the smile left Caroline's lips, and Mary dropped her teaspoon.

She bent to pick it up; but, before she could do so, he had forestalled her, and was offering her another from the tray.

She mumbled her thanks, avoiding his glance. He sat down, and addressed Mrs. Arkwright.

"Well, ma'am? I'll wager you didn't expect to see me, eh?"

It was at once evident that he was in a good humour. Caroline's quick, birdlike glance darted towards him, and the smile returned to her face.

"That I didn't, Will," returned Mrs. Arkwright. "You'll take a dish of tea—or are you in a hurry?"

"I can spare a few moments," she said, accepting the offer with a nod.

He leaned back in his chair at ease, and watched her pouring the tea. The sun glinted briefly through the parlour windows, adding a touch of Spring to the domestic scene.

"You're snug in here," he said, looking around him contentedly. "You females lead a pleasant life, by and large."

"Well, you may think so, Will," replied Mrs. Arkwright. "But I don't mind telling you that one can have a little too much of peace and quiet. If the weather hadn't turned for the better so that I could get out and about a bit, I should have been moped to death, I declare!"

He laughed. "You, moped to death, ma'am! That is something I should like to see. You are the most cheerful female of my acquaintance." He paused, seemingly struck by a sudden thought. "Should you like to give an evening party? You are always saying that we don't entertain enough, and I have something to celebrate at present."

"A party!" Two voices took up the chorus eagerly.

"Not you, young lady." He turned a sober look on Caroline. "You've not earned a party. Besides you're too young, in any case."

The fact that she uttered no protest spoke much for the repentant frame of Caroline's mind at present. Arkwright's lips twitched, but he managed to check the smile.

"Whom will you ask, Will?" demanded Mrs. Arkwright. "Shall we have dancing? Do you think we should ask the Colonel and Miss Grey, or will they consider themselves above our neighbours? I dare say we could muster fifteen couple, and we often used to have as many as that in this room at one time, when your poor father was alive——"

"Not so fast!" he said, laughing. "I had nothing so ambitious in mind as a large party, with dancing. I thought we might perhaps ask a few of our more intimate friends—the Colonel and Miss Grey certainly, if they will honour us; my father's friends, the Shaws, from Dewsbury; the Websters, whom you visited yesterday; the doctor and his wife—oh and Miss Lister—with, of course, her uncle."

Mary jumped. "Oh, I——" she stumbled a little over her words—"thank you—you are very kind. I shall be glad to come and sit with Caroline. As for my uncle—I do not quite know what—it depends, of course, when it is to be."

"You'll do no such thing," he said, in a downright tone. "As sit with Caro, I mean."

"Oh, but——" she paused, helplessly. "Indeed, I'd prefer to," she finished.

"No doubt. But, like Caroline, you have some expiation to make." He looked at her in no unkindly way. "If Caro is barred from the party, and you are deprived of the opportunity of sitting with her, I think the purpose of discipline will be served. Her social instinct and your maternal one will alike have to make a sacrifice."

Mary looked away: she felt herself blushing. Mrs. Arkwright came to her rescue.

"Yes, when is it to be, Will?" she demanded, eagerly. "Of course, I would have liked a larger party—but perhaps later on, when the nights are lighter, and Caro's foot is better—not that there is much wrong with it, now, only you say that she shall not—and, of course, you are right," she added, hastily, catching his eye. "There'll not be much preparation needed for a small affair of this nature—they will take their mutton with us, I suppose, and then we shall play cards, or the young ladies will sing, or something of that kind——"

"Must I eat my dinner alone in the schoolroom?" asked Caroline, in a very small voice. "Or may I have it with Nellie?"

He looked at her in silence for a moment, considering.

"You may eat your dinner with the company," he conceded, at last. "But you will retire immediately afterwards—understood?"

Her face lit up. "Oh, Will! You are so good, and I shall not mind a bit——"

She broke off, biting her lip. He laughed.

"Be careful, or I may need to think of some other way of impressing your fault upon you. Well, that's settled." He put down his tea-cup, and rose to go. "As for the time—why, tomorrow, I think. There seems no point in delay."

"Tomorrow!" Mrs. Arkwright looked startled. "But isn't that—oh, well," she continued, "as I said, there'll not be much preparation needed. I'll see Nell later on, and we'll soon set everything in train. It's a pity that daffodils are so late this year—I wonder what Caro should wear—the pink muslin, perhaps——"

"This is no place for me," he said, laughing. "Settle it among yourselves—I'm off."

"But, Will," asked Caroline, puzzled. "What is it you want to celebrate by giving a party?"

"Oh, that." He paused on his way to the door. "The future of the mill, and the expansion of our trade. I have my new shearing frames installed. They arrived safely last night."

He nodded, and passed out of the room.

13

An Evening Party

MARY'S HANDS TREMBLED slightly as she fastened the small buttons at the back of her simple yellow muslin gown. She picked up the locket that contained miniatures of her parents, and clasped its slim chain about her neck. This done, she surveyed herself anxiously in the ancient spotted mirror that stood on her dressing table.

Her russet hair was piled high on top of her head, exposing her small ears to view more than was usual. For a moment she toyed with the idea of pulling it all down again, and doing it more in her everyday style. After all, she was only the governess, and Mr. Arkwright might think it a liberty for her to dress like his other female guests. But just then her uncle knocked quietly on the door to signify that he was ready, so there was no time to alter anything. She snatched up the fine white woollen shawl which had been lovingly fashioned for her by her mother, seized her reticule and gloves, and hurried from the room.

They were conveyed to the Arkwrights' house in Dr. Walker's carriage; the doctor and his wife lived not far from the Vicarage, and had kindly offered to take up Mr. Booth and his niece. John, who had not been included in the invitation, saw them off with a solemn face. Mary had not found many opportunities of talking alone with him lately; but she knew that he was disturbed by the arrival of yet another consignment of shearing frames to Arkwright's mill. News of this event had spread throughout the district with alarming rapidity.

Somewhat surprisingly, the Greys had accepted William Arkwright's invitation. When she set eyes on Lucinda, Mary wished heartily that they had not. Miss Grey always looked lovely: tonight, in a blue satin shot with gold, she certainly surpassed herself. She wore a narrow sequined ribbon threaded through her shining golden curls, and this enhanced her usual regal air. At the side of her, Mary felt positively dowdy.

Lucinda greeted her with a nod of immense distance, which prompted Mrs. Shaw, an old friend of the Arkwrights, to ask Mrs. Arkwright who was that beautiful, stuck-up girl in the blue.

"That's Miss Grey—I'll present her to you just now, my dear," promised Mrs. Arkwright, resplendent in purple and lace. "She's Colonel Grey's daughter, and, of course, they move in the best society in York, so it's a great honour to have her here at all."

"Happen it is," said forthright Mrs. Shaw, with a sniff. "But she means us to know it, don't she? Myself, I reckon more to that little lass in yellow—Caro's governess, isn't she?"

Mrs. Arkwright nodded. "Yes; you must meet her, too. Oh, here come the Websters! I must go and welcome them."

"I'll come, too," replied Mrs. Shaw. "I don't need to stand on ceremony with Martha Webster, for I've known her ever since I can remember. I wonder when that boy of theirs means to take a wife? He's five and twenty now, and no sign of anything serious. I don't know what ails the lads nowadays—take your Will, for instance."

"Oh, Will's not the marrying kind," said Mrs. Arkwright, bustling towards the newcomers.

Mrs. Shaw shot a shrewd glance at Arkwright, who was at that moment talking to Lucinda Grey with earnest attention.

"All men's the marrying kind—think on," she said, meaningly.

But fortunately, Mrs. Arkwright was too involved in

her duties as a hostess to heed the words of a very old friend.

Altogéther, they numbered sixteen at the dinner table, including the family. The Colonel and Lucinda sat one on each side of Arkwright, who was in his place at the head of the table. Mrs. Arkwright sat at the foot with Caroline on one side of her, and Mr. Booth and his niece on the other. Mary found that Arthur Webster had been placed on her right; he was a pleasant, easy-going young man who looked after her diligently, and soon coaxed her into laughing.

"You're not from Yorkshire, are you, Miss Lister?" he asked her, after a time.

"No—how did you guess?"

"You haven't the twang—and your voice is softer. Our women have loud voices, for the most part."

"But warm hearts," retorted Mary.

"Oh, as to hearts, ma'am, I can't say. I've no experience in such matters, more's the pity."

"Indeed?" She smiled incredulously.

"I see you don't believe me, but I assure you it's true. I'm still hoping to meet someone who will instruct me. Now, you're a governess, Miss Lister——"

"You're absurd," she said, smiling faintly. It was impossible to take him seriously, but she did not quite like him to flirt with her so openly on such a short acquaintance. "Mrs. Arkwright is trying to catch your attention."

While Arthur Webster was talking to his hostess, Mary let her glance wander to the other end of the table. She was surprised to find that Arkwright was staring straight at her, a disapproving frown on his brow. For a moment, their eyes met; Mary's dropped before his, and to her discomfiture, she felt a blush rising. What was wrong? Did he think she was forgetting her place in chatting too freely with one of his guests? Or did he disapprove of the interest which Mr. Webster was showing in her, believing that she had encouraged it? Either way, she thought ruefully, he evidently judged her conduct unbecoming.

"You're very quiet," teased Arthur Webster, returning to the attack as Mrs. Arkwright turned her attention elsewhere. "A penny for them."

"They wouldn't be worth it," returned Mary, with a quick glance down the table again.

He noticed the movement, and looked in the same direction.

"Don't let our friend Arkwright put you off," he said, guessing her thoughts with uncomfortable precision. "After all, he's been amusing himself until this very moment in the most enviable way."

"I—I don't know what you mean," said Mary.

He gave her a quizzical glance. "Don't you, ma'am? But just wait a moment—there, look now! What did I tell you?"

She looked again, and was unable to take her eyes away for several minutes. Arkwright was bending over to talk to Lucinda Grey; the dark head and the fair one were very close together, their attitude suggestive of a tender intimacy that brought a quick pang to Mary.

In that moment, she made a surprising and most unwelcome discovery.

"Well, don't stare them out of countenance," whispered her lively neighbour. "Have some fellow feeling, eh?"

Mary bestowed a brief, vague smile on him, and forced herself to ignore what was going forward at the head of the table.

The meal was drawing to a close, and the final course was laid before the guests. A babble of talk and laughter filled the room; eyes were bright, and faces animated. Mrs. Arkwright looked around her with a complacent smile, and thought how pleasant it all was, and that they must certainly do it again soon.

And then the smile froze on her face.

A sudden crash of shattering glass broke into the cheerful buzz of conversation: it was followed by a dull thud as something landed on the carpet underneath the windows, not far from the dining table.

The chatter died away. Several of the women uttered half-stifled shrieks. Arkwright jumped up from his seat, brushing past Lucinda almost roughly as he made his way to the spot where the object lay. He stooped and picked it up: it was a heavy stone.

He pulled back the curtain from the unshuttered window, releasing a shower of glass splinters. There was a large jagged hole in the window pane where the stone had passed through.

He dropped the stone, and dashed from the room. Colonel Grey threw down his napkin and followed him almost at once.

An uneasy murmur of voices arose, and one of the younger lady guests, Louisa Shaw, burst into tears. Her husband bent over her, whispering words of comfort in her ear. Caroline looked for a moment as though she might follow young Mrs. Shaw's example.

"What is it, Mama?" she asked, in a frightened whisper.

"Nothing, love," asserted Mrs. Arkwright, with a stoutness of heart she certainly did not feel. "Just some lads playing about, I dare say—your brother'll soon teach them a lesson, you mark my words."

"Do you really think it's that?" demanded Caroline, doubtfully.

"Well, I don't, for one," said Arthur Webster quietly to Mary. "When my father told me that Will Arkwright had got some more shearing frames, I knew there'd be trouble."

"You don't think——" the colour receded from her cheeks.

"Nay, who can say? All the same, if you'll excuse me, I think I'll just see if I can lend a hand out there."

It seemed that several of the men had formed a similar intention, for they began to rise.

This brought an immediate outcry from their womenfolk. "Don't go and leave us alone!"

Dr. Webster took charge. "You young fellows go," he directed. "The rest of us will stay with the ladies, unless you call for us."

Pretty little Louisa Shaw began to cry with renewed vigour at the threat of losing her husband: but her mother-in-law took her firmly but gently in hand, while she signalled quietly to Tom to do as the doctor suggested. He and Arthur Webster went quickly from the room.

"Well, there's no sense in the rest of us sitting here," said Mrs. Arkwright, trying desperately to rally the party. "Our pudding's spoilt, so why don't we all go into the parlour, and Nell will bring us a few of her cheesecakes, and some sugared plums. The gentlemen can bring the decanter along with them, and we shall all be comfortable again. Louisa, my dear, perhaps you would be the better for a very little—just a spot, you know—of port wine in some warm water——"

Louisa thanked her hostess tearfully, but said she really could not bring herself to take anything of that nature.

"Oh, well, you know best, child," replied her hostess. "Shall we move, then?"

Everyone seemed agreed on this, and the change was quickly made. But the spirit had gone out of the party. Mrs. Arkwright did her best, ably aided by Mary; but the tempting sweetmeats which they pressed on the guests were refused, and only the level of the decanter showed signs of appreciation.

"I'll have the tea-tray brought in," whispered Mrs. Arkwright to Mary. "It's too early, really, but the ladies need a stimulant more than the men do, I reckon, and they're punishing the port handsomely."

"Should we try some music?" suggested Mary.

Mrs. Arkwright brightened. "A good idea, Miss Lister! I'll ask Miss Grey to sing to us; for, upon my word, she's as cool as a cucumber—not a bit put out."

Lucinda was willing, in her calm, assured way, to oblige the company. Mary offered to play for her; and, after the usual preliminaries of selection were over, they both applied themselves to the task of entertaining a more than usually difficult audience.

After a time, the atmosphere grew calmer. Young Mrs. Shaw, fortified by tea and the smelling-bottle, dried her eyes, and was able to listen to Miss Grey's song with the appearance of attention. It was just finishing when male voices were heard in the hall, and a moment later the party of men, headed by Arkwright, burst into the room.

"Any luck?" asked Mr. Shaw, senior.

Arkwright shook his head. "Whoever did it has either got clean away, or is in hiding somewhere close at hand. I'm inclined to favour the first—he had five minutes' start of us, and knew where he was making for, which gave him a decided advantage."

"Hiding somewhere?" echoed Mrs. Webster, nervously; while Louisa Shaw showed signs of breaking down again.

"No, I don't really think so," replied the mill-owner, looking round at the ladies with a reassuring air. "In any case, I've set the men on to keep a sharp look-out, so you've nothing to fear."

Colonel Grey added the weight of his opinion to this pronouncement, and Mr. Tom Shaw went to sit by his wife's side.

"Well," continued Arkwright, "we mustn't allow this unfortunate incident to spoil our whole evening, must we? Miss Grey, we seem to have interrupted your song. If you will pardon our somewhat dishevelled state, perhaps we can prevail upon you to favour us with another?"

Mrs. Arkwright seconded this appeal, and several of the men also took it up: but it was evident that a mood of uneasiness had settled over the party, particularly among the women. Excuses were brought up which made an early start for home desirable; some mentioned the fact that there was a good deal of cloud tonight obscuring the moon.

At last, Miss Grey did give one more song in a style that was faultless, yet failed to make much impression on her audience. No one seemed inclined to follow her example; and once again, the excuses began to be heard.

Arkwright applied to young Mrs. Shaw, but she shook her head, begging in a faint voice to be excused, as she feared her nerves were too greatly overset at present.

"We'd best get her home," said Mrs. Shaw, senior. "Bella, love——" to Mrs. Arkwright—"you'll forgive us, I'm sure."

"Oh, but you can't go yet, Mrs. Shaw!" protested

the incorrigible Arthur Webster. "Miss Lister will sing for us, won't you ma'am? I'm sure you'll not wish to go until you've heard her," he added, turning to Mrs. Shaw again.

Mary declined hastily, not at all happy at being thrust into notice. But Arthur Webster, faced with the prospect of an abrupt ending to what he had found a pleasant evening, was determined. He picked up a book of duets from the pianoforte, and handed it to Mary.

"There, ma'am, you choose one, and I'll sing it with you. I know most of these."

"Ay, a capital notion!" approved Arthur's father.

"As you say, Webster," remarked Arkwright, dryly, "capital."

Mary glanced quickly at him, and was surprised to catch a flash of anger in his dark eyes. It was gone in a moment.

She had no choice but to sing, however, for several people pressed the pair: and the next half hour or so was agreeably passed by everyone except Louisa Shaw and Mary herself. She found Arthur Webster's liveliness a constant source of embarrassment. His part in the song frequently had an amorous tone, and he put plenty of expression into it, causing her to be thankful for the need to keep her eyes on the music. She felt, rather than saw, her employer's disapproval.

At last, it was over; and now all efforts to keep the party going were useless. A general exodus began.

Waiting on the step for the doctor's carriage, Mary saw William Arkwright take his leave of the Greys. He seemed to linger unnecessarily over the business of handing in Lucinda, and stood looking after the carriage as it drove away. In contrast, he took a very curt leave of herself, barely acknowledging her softly spoken goodnight.

Her spirits were low on the homeward journey. It was fortunate that no one else felt in the mood for conversation, or her silence must have been noticed. The doctor deposited her uncle and herself at the Vicarage gate, and they walked silently up the path together.

As they reached the door and Mr. Booth raised the

knocker, Mary chanced to look back towards the gate.
While she watched, a figure glided out of the shadows,
and through the gate into the road. It was too far away
for her to see more than an outline, but she recognized
it at once, with a quick alarm.

It was Black George Mellor.

14

The Letter

ARKWRIGHT WAS EARLY at the mill next morning. He
summoned Nick Bradley.

"You had a quiet night, I suppose, Nick, or I should
have had warning?"

The overseer nodded. "Not a sound, after tha looked
in. Didst cop t' chap who flung t' stone?"

His employer shook his head. "No. He got away,
whoever he was. Any ideas, Nick?"

Bradley pursed his lips. "Reckon it might've been
Hartley—but, then, again, could be any o' t' Ludds, for
that matter. There can't have been more nor one of
'em, or they'd have done more damage, think on."

"Yes, that's my own view. I look on it as an isolated
gesture of defiance—as you say, possibly from Hartley.
But once I realized that the miscreant wasn't anywhere
around the house, I thought it best to come over and
make sure that you hadn't had an attack on the mill. I
don't mind admitting, Nick, that I had a nasty moment
thinking of the machines, when I saw that stone come
through the window." He paused, and Bradley nodded.
"We must continue to mount guard here, for the time
being, I'm afraid. Can you arrange to sleep here again
for the next couple of nights? We'll take it turn and
turn about. And I've another idea—I'll borrow one of
the dogs from my friend Shaw's farm. You can turn it

loose in the mill after dark, and it should give warning if anyone's about. How are the machines going?"

"T' machines is a' reight," replied Nick, darkly.

"What do you mean?"

"It's t' lads," admitted the overseer, after a struggle. "Some of 'em tries to go slow on t' machines, so's not to show up t' hand croppers."

"If anyone tries that, he's to go at once, do you hear?" snapped Arkwright, rising hastily. "I'll go in there myself."

Bradley shook his head. "Reckon tha'd best not turn off any more chaps, at present, Maister Will. T' would do a power o' harm, what wi' machines, and all."

"I may have to," returned his master. "For a time, at least. Later on, of course, when we get more work into the mill—as we shall, now that we've the means of tackling a greater quantity—I hope not only to keep the numbers, but to increase them. But I can't afford to pay idle men, Nick, even for a short period. You know that as well as anyone."

"Ay. All t' same, Maister Will, it might turn out cheaper in t' long run. Bide tha time; and if go they must, let it be one by one, not all at once."

"It goes against the grain, b'God!" said Arkwright. "Why, in my grandfather's time—ay, and my father's—a man had the running of his own manufactory, and would no more have thought of pandering to the notions of his workmen than he would have of taking wings to the moon!"

"Times is changin'," replied Bradley, shaking his head. "And when all's said, they're human beings, think on. A cropper's proud o' his skill, an' now wi' t' coming o' they machines, his work's not wanted. How'd tha like that, thysen? Reckon their pride hurts 'em nigh as much as bein' out o' work—there's more things can pinch a man nor his belly, think on."

"Yes," said Arkwright, thoughtfully. "I know."

For the rest of the morning, he was fully occupied. At midday, he began to feel hungry, and decided to return to the house for a meal. This was not usual: often he would work throughout the day, returning home only as daylight began to fail, when work in the mill had to stop.

His arrival set the house in a bustle. Nellie rushed away to hurry the meal on to the table, while Mrs. Arkwright deplored the fact that they had been about to sit down to nothing more interesting than a slice or two of cold ham.

"I want nothing more, ma'am," he said, laughing. "I often manage on less, as you very well know."

"Yes, but—if only you had said, this morning, that you meant to return, Will! I could have got Nellie to bake a mutton pie——"

"I imagine we shall eat a good dinner as usual, this evening?" he asked.

"To be sure, Will—but——"

"Very well, then. And now, ma'am, I would like to read my newspaper. Perhaps there is something you should be doing?"

She took the hint, and was about to leave him alone; but at the door she paused, suddenly remembering something.

"Oh! Will——" she said, picking up a folded note which lay on a side-table, and taking it over to him— "I nearly forgot. This came for you—at least, it didn't exactly come——"

He stared at the note, not heeding her words. It bore his name in rough capitals, and nothing else. He frowned, and unfolded it in one swift, impatient movement. His eyes came to rest on the brief message it contained, and seemed as though fixed. His face turned first red, then white. Mrs. Arkwright looked at him in alarm.

"What is it——?"

He jumped to his feet, screwed the paper into a ball, and flung it away from him across the room. His eyes were blazing. He turned fiercely on her.

"How did this come here? Who brought it? Who brought it, d' you hear?"

"Why, I was telling you, Will," she stammered, taken aback by his vehemence. "We don't rightly know. Miss Lister found it in her pocket, not long since—I thought of sending one of the lads down to the mill with it for you, but then it didn't seem all that important—a nasty, dirty bit of paper, and such a scrawl on it as I never did see—I thought——"

"Miss Lister? Miss Lister, you say? Found it—*in her pocket*?"

He repeated the words incredulously, as though he thought her mad.

She nodded, half afraid of his wild look.

"Send Miss Lister to me," he ordered, peremptorily.

"What is it, Will?" she ventured to ask. "What is it that's put you about so?"

"Later." He waved her away. "Send Miss Lister here."

She went, not knowing what to make of it, but realizing that this was not the moment for questioning him. He would tell her in his own good time.

A few moments later, Mary entered the room, looking slightly puzzled. She had not been able to make much of Mrs. Arkwright's gabbled explanation, but she had gathered that Mr. Arkwright was upset over something to do with the letter.

"This note." He strode across the room, retrieved the paper, and held it towards her, clenched in his fist. "How did it get here?"

"I found it in my pocket," replied Mary, steadily. She knew that it sounded absurd, but it was the truth. "I took off my pelisse this morning when I arrived, and felt in the pocket for a handkerchief. It was then that I found the note."

"Why did you not notice it before—when you first put on the garment, for instance?"

She looked curiously into his pale, set face. It was evident that he was keeping a tight rein on what she guessed was a white-hot anger. What could be wrong?

"I can't really say. I had no occasion to feel in my pocket, then. It is not a very large piece of paper."

"And you seriously expect me to believe that you found it in your pocket?"

"Of course I do." She took slight exception to his tone. "It happens to be true—though I know it sounds ridiculous. I cannot imagine how it should come to be there."

"I must confess I can think of only one way, Miss Lister." She looked a question. "That you put it there yourself," he finished, with biting emphasis.

"But I did not!" she cried, indignantly. "Haven't I told you so, Mr. Arkwright?"

"Oh, yes. But you can't suppose I am fool enough to believe it."

For a moment, she was deprived of speech.

"What are you saying?" she demanded, at last, her anger rising. "Are you suggesting that I am—lying to you?"

He nodded curtly. "Yes," he said. "I'm suggesting that—exactly."

"Upon my word, I think you must have run mad!" she retorted, flinging caution to the winds. "Why should I lie to you about such a—such a stupid matter?"

"Do you know what is in this note?" he asked.

She shook her head. "I neither know nor care! What concerns me, is that you should credit me with——"

"Stuff!" he said, fiercely. "Injured innocence will not carry this off, ma'am! You have brought me a warning letter from the Luddites—now tell me you found it in your pocket!"

She fell back a pace, and stared. "Was that what it was?" she asked, in an awed whisper.

"Ay, that's what it was. Get rid of my machines, or they'll do it for me—that's what they threaten. And it's signed 'General Snipshears'! A friend of yours, no doubt, since he leaves his billet doux in your pocket?"

His mouth was twisted into a sneer. She looked at him in bewilderment; anyone less angry than he was at that moment must have seen that she knew nothing of the letter.

"I suppose that damned cousin of yours gave it you to deliver," he went on, unpleasantly. "He wrote it most likely."

"No!"

"No?" he mocked. "But I dare say you know who did?"

"Of course I do not!" She was angry again. "I know nothing whatever about it, except what I've already

told you. As for John—that's not his handwriting, as
you can surely guess. That is a rough, untutored
hand——"

"Such things would be written in a disguised hand.
No man in his senses would betray himself like that."

"Well, I tell you, sir, that John had nothing whatever to do with this. He is opposed to all violence, and
threats of violence. Why, when he agreed to head the
deputation of workmen that came to see you, it was
only on condition that it should be a peaceable mission——"

"Did you know about that beforehand?"

"Why, yes. I did. It was purely by chance——"

She stopped, realizing that it was unwise to say
more. He noticed her hesitation, and pounced on it.

"If you knew of that, then it's odds on you know
something about this. Come, Miss Lister!" He drew
nearer to her, looking down on her threateningly. "We
will have the truth now, if you please, and no more
beating about the bush."

She drew herself up to her full height, and gave him
back look for look, though her knees trembled a little.

"You've had the truth!" she flung at him. "If you
think to browbeat me, you are very much mistaken,
sir! Neither I nor my cousin can tell you anything more
about that letter."

She made such a spirited picture, standing there with
flushed cheeks and eyes that sparkled with anger, that
a flash of admiration came into his eyes. It was gone in
a moment.

"It's no good, ma'am. You may play off all those
pretty feminine wiles with which you were beguiling
young Webster yesterday evening——"

"How dare you insult me so?" She was almost
speechless with indignation.

"Did you suppose I hadn't noticed?" he asked,
sneering again. "As far as that goes, I dare say all the
company must have done so—it was plain enough."

"How could you?" Her voice broke a little. "It is ungentlemanlike of you——"

"You forget, Miss Lister—I am not a gentleman.

And if you may act in an unwomanly way, I feel at liberty to act in an unmanly one."

"I did not! Mr. Webster is one of these gay, light-hearted people—he meant nothing, as I very well know——"

"The more shame——"

But this was too much for Mary. "I will not be catechised by you!" she said, stamping her foot. "You may be my employer, but you have no right to question my behaviour in personal affairs. I—I will not tolerate it, sir!"

"You won't, eh?" He seized her suddenly by the arms, and glared down into her face. "Then, b'God, I'll not tolerate you in my house any longer! You can go now, Miss Lister—this very minute!"

His words had the effect he desired. The fire died out of Mary's face, leaving it pale.

"Do you mean that?" she asked, in a whisper.

"I've never meant anything more. I consider you an undesirable influence for my sister. Not only is your behaviour unmaidenly, but it's also plain to me that you and your cousin are as near to being Ludds as makes no odds. My house will be the better for your going."

For a moment she said nothing, staring at him with a stricken look which began to pierce his anger. Then she turned away, moving unsteadily towards the door.

"Very well, sir—if that is your wish. I will go now." She paused for a moment. "You—perhaps—you will—explain to Caro——" Her voice broke on the name. She put her hand quickly in front of her face, and ran from the room.

She did not quite know how, but she managed to leave the house without meeting anyone. She made her way blindly home, and, entering the empty parlour, flung herself down on the sofa. Then, at last, she could give way to the tears that were choking her.

"Mary! Why, Mary, my dear girl, whatever's amiss?"

It was her cousin's voice. She answered him with a low moan. He came to her side, and put his arm about her. For a few moments, they clung together as they had done in childhood over a shared sorrow.

"Poor little love!" he said, presently. "Won't you tell me what's wrong?"

Between sobs, she began to tell him: but she had gone no further than the letter, when he stopped her with an exclamation.

"In your pocket? A letter from the Ludds?"

She nodded, mopping her eyes with her soaked handkerchief.

"Mary, I think I know how it came there." He began to stutter. "G-George was here last n-night. He brought that letter, and w-wanted me to—to—ask you——"

She raised her tear-stained face, and stared at him. "Not to ask me to deliver it?"

He nodded. "Yes. And I refused, of course. He t-turned nasty, then, and said I must t-take it myself. We—we argued, and must have made t-too much noise, for Mrs. Duckworth came down to see what w-was wrong. George hid in the c-closet where w-we hang our outdoor things—I expect he did it then."

"Yes, my pelisse was hanging in there. But——" she was calmer now, as her mind began to grapple with the present problem—"so was Mrs. Duckworth's. How could he be sure——"

"Oh, Mary!" He gave a little laugh, the absurdity of what she had said breaking through his distress. "Why, any garment of Mrs. Duckworth's would go around you twice! There could be no mistaking yours."

"I suppose not." She sighed heavily. "What a dreadful man that is! I wish—oh, how I wish, John—that you'd never become involved with him."

"He's not so bad, you know, only—desperate, and determined to do something for the workers. In his own way, he's been a friend to me."

"Not my notion of a friend," said Mary bitterly. "All your troubles—and now mine, too—come from him."

"Why, Mary? What happened when you found the letter? Did you give it to Arkwright? You have not told me."

"Yes, I gave it to him." She was able to talk calmly now, though her face still showed the ravages of emotion. "You can imagine how angry he was—he said all kinds of hurtful, unkind things——"

"Don't heed them, love." He patted her hand. "Arkwright's a hasty man, but he's not bad at heart. Tomorrow he'll realize that he's done you an injustice, and beg your pardon—you see if he doesn't."

"There'll be no tomorrow," replied Mary, pressing her lips firmly together to stop them trembling. "He has dismissed me."

"Dismissed you!" John jumped to his feet, his expression indignant. "Dismissed you—*you*! But this is—is—rank injustice!"

"I told him that. But he said that he thought I was a bad influence on Caroline, as both of us—you and I—are close to being Luddites ourselves."

"Not as close as we could be, though!" John replied, slowly.

He stood still for a moment, lost in thought.

Presently, he roused himself. "George is right," he said, in a determined manner. "I must either be with them or against them—there is no middle way. At present, I'm trusted by neither side—I scarce can trust myself, at times." He paused. "There's a meeting tonight at the St. Crispin Inn, in Halifax. He told me of it last night, and wanted me to go. I think I shall."

"No!" Mary rose hastily, and took his arm. "Don't, I beg you, John! Don't do anything you will regret—especially not on my account."

"It's not only you, lass, it's everything. Poor Sam Hartley, and others like him—and Arkwright secure in his autocracy, refusing to heed others or to negotiate with anyone——"

"Please, John. For my sake, don't go," she pleaded. "What is this meeting? Is it——"

"Never mind what it is, Mary. You'd best know nothing more." He paused, then continued, "What will you tell my father?"

"I don't know." She had been wondering about this herself. "What can I tell him? I daren't mention the letter, or he must learn of that man's visit last night. And whatever I tell him, he will most likely go and see

Mr. Arkwright about it, in any case. What can I do, John?"

"Leave it for the present," he advised. "Is there anywhere you can go for this afternoon, so that you would return at the usual time?"

"I could go for a walk," she said, doubtfully. "It is quite mild today. Why don't you come with me, and then we can talk things over, and decide what I had best do? I suppose——" she gulped—"I suppose I must look about me for another post."

"My father may know of someone."

She shook her head. "Not here—I want to go away, nearer to my own home. Not that I am ungrateful——"

She could not finish the words.

"It is infamous!" declared John, moved by her attempts to conceal her distress. "I begin to feel that Arkwright is no better than the Ludds think him, after all."

She shook her head. "No," she said, with difficulty. "He—oh, you cannot understand. Whatever he may do, I can never think ill of him."

15

Bradley Brings a Warning

APART FROM SAYING curtly that Miss Lister had been obliged to go home because she felt indisposed, Arkwright ate his meal in silence and speedily returned to the mill.

There he summoned the spy McDonald, locked the door of his office, and questioned the man closely. Afterwards he sent for Nick Bradley.

He told him briefly about the letter. The overseer shook his head.

"Reckon 'twas bound to happen, Maister. They've sworn to smash all t' machines in t' neighbourhood."

"We'll see about that," returned Arkwright grimly.

Nick scratched his head. "I'm in a rare puzzle to know how yon letter got into Miss Lister's pocket. She'd have nowt to do wi' it, as we well knows."

"Do we?"

Nick stared. "Nay, lad, surely tha don't think——"

"Why not? Both she and that precious cousin of hers make no secret of their sympathy with the working folk."

"Ay, but sympathy's one thing, an' threatenin' folks wi' violence is another, lad. That little lass! As soon suspect my Annie o' it."

"Well, capable of it or not, I can't risk having Luddite sympathizers under my own roof. She's gone."

"What? Tha's never given her t' push?" asked Nick, incredulously. "An 'er not long come, an' like as not short o' brass, too? An' all for a letter which anyone might 'ave shoved in 'er pocket? I'd not 'ave thought it o' thee, Maister Will, I tell thee straight!"

Arkwright had the grace to look a trifle hangdog.

"I can't afford to take risks, Nick, as you know only too well."

"Ay, risks—but yon lass——"

"That'll do. You're an old servant, but you can't manage my affairs for me. Enough of that. Tell me, do you know anything of a so-called Democratic Club which is held at the St. Crispin, in Halifax?"

Nick hesitated for a moment. "Ay. Leastways, I've 'eard tell on 't."

"What kind of organization is it—could it be a cover for the Luddites, think you?"

Nick shook his head. "Nay, don't ask me, Maister. I tak' my ale in Liversedge at t' Shears Inn, same as most lads."

"But you must have heard some talk in the mill," insisted Arkwright. "McDonald has just been with me, and he reports that he overheard some of the men talking about a meeting of this Club to be held in the St. Crispin tonight at eight o'clock. When he asked them about it, they said he'd been mistaken—there was no such Club in existence nowadays."

"Sithee, Maister, tha's got one spy in t' mill. Reckon that's enough."

"Look, Nick. That threatening letter may have been simply a childish attempt to scare me. But assuming that it meant business, any meeting in the neighbourhood at present is suspect. If you know anything at all, it's your duty to tell me."

"Duty!" Bradley sighed heavily. "I wish I did know what's my duty, an' that's a fact! It's nigh impossible at times, what wi' tryin' to do reight by t' lads an' by thee, Maister Will. This much I can say—when last I 'eard owt on t' Club, 'twas that some on t' members had left on account o' goings on as they didn't 'old with. Don't ask me what, for I don't know, and likely wouldn't say if I did."

"Then it's still in existence?"

"As far as I know."

"Very well," said Arkwright, decisively. "I'll see Colonel Grey and get him to send some men over to the St. Crispin tonight. You've convinced me that I shan't be wasting his time."

"Don't put it on me, Maister. It may be all for nowt, an' God knows I've no wish to bring t' Redcoats down on lads who're doin no one any 'arm——"

"All right, Nick." Arkwright nodded in dismissal. "But perhaps I'm not as blind as you think to the difficulties of your situation. You're not the only one to be pulled in two directions at once."

Bradley went back to his work with a troubled mind. Presently he saw Arkwright leaving the mill, and guessed his master was bound for Colonel Grey's home in Halifax. His uneasiness grew. He had no certain knowledge that any of his men were to be present at this meeting, but it was a possibility that filled him with anxiety. There was someone else who might be there, too; someone, though foolish, as yet innocent of any crime. His arrest would bring suffering to those even more innocent than himself. A half-formed intention came into the overseer's mind.

He tried to thrust it away, telling himself that it would be disloyal to his master, but gradually it gained ground. By the time he had seen the last man off the premises and locked the mill door, he had made up his mind.

He walked briskly over to the Vicarage. Mrs. Duckworth opened the door to him, telling him to be quick and state his business, as she had something in the oven. He asked to see John.

"He's out, nor not expected back all night," she told him. "T' Reverend's abroad, too. There's only Miss Mary, and she's lying down on her bed with a bad headache, poor lamb. Won't it wait till tomorrow?"

"Reckon it'll have to——" began Nick, reluctantly, when footsteps sounded on the stairs.

Mary's pale face peered over the housekeeper's shoulder. "I heard your voice asking for John," she said, coming forward. "Is there anything I can do for you instead?"

"You shouldn't have come down, Miss Mary. But if you can see to it now you're here——"

Mrs. Duckworth bustled gratefully back to the kitchen.

Mary asked Nick inside, and closed the door. "How can I help you?"

He shuffled uneasily. "I don't know as tha can—leastways——"

"There isn't anything wrong, is there?"

He hesitated. "Happen not. But dost know where Maister John's gone tonight?"

"No, I——" She broke off suddenly, her eyes widening in fear. "Now I think of it, he did say something—but I was upset at the time, and didn't pay much heed. He mentioned some meeting in Halifax——"

"That's what I came about," said Nick, heavily. "Dost reckon he's gone there, Miss?"

Her face grew paler still. "I—I think it likely. Why? You know something, I can see. What is it, Nick? Why have you come to see John?"

"I wanted to drop a friendly word o' warning, that's all. Reckon 'tis too late now."

"Too late?" She clutched his arm. "What do you know? Is John in any danger? Tell me, I beg you!"

"Least said, soonest mended, Miss. If t' lad's gone to t' St. Crispin, there's nowt either on us can do. Reckon he's played wi' fire once too often—I knowed how t'would be."

"For God's sake, tell me!"

"Happen I shouldn't," he said doubtfully. "Though it's hard to see t' innocent suffer wi' t' guilty—not that there's owt to be done that I can see. It's like this—t' Redcoats are goin' to t' St. Crispin tonight—Maister Arkwright reckons as it's a Luddite meeting, an' he's warned Colonel Grey."

Mary pressed her hands to her head distractedly. "I must think. There must be some way—what time is it now?"

"Close on six——"

"Then there might be time!" She seized his arm energetically. "I recollect he said this meeting was for eight o'clock. If I can reach the inn before him—quick, Nick! How can I get there in time?"

"Tha's never meanin' to go there thysen?"

"Who else would go? John would not wish my uncle to know of this, and there's no one else. But how shall I get there? Think, think!"

"B' God!" exclaimed the overseer. "If ever I seed a lass wi' t' spunk o' a lad, 'tis thysen! Ay, reckon I can find summat to get thee there—but how wilt go on, then? He'll be wi' all that lot—an' a reight rough lot they are, an' no mistake. 'Tis man's work, lass." He paused. "I'll go for thee."

Her eyes filled with tears. "You're a true friend, Nick. But it won't answer—John can be very obstinate when he's excited, and I don't think he'd pay attention to anyone but me. I must do everything possible—I must go myself."

"Then I'll go along o' thee," said Bradley quietly. "There's a gig I can borrow. We can be in Halifax just turned seven, and keep a look out at t' Crispin for thy cousin. Please God we'll catch him in time." He paused. "What'll tha tell t' good woman in there?"

"I must give her a hint that John's in danger—she knows how he involves himself in these matters," replied Mary. "She'll think of something to tell my uncle that will not alarm him."

"Then get about it, lass, while I fetch t' gig. An' wrap up warm, mind, for 'tis sharp tonight." He turned to go, then paused. "Happen what I'm doin' is wrong," he said, slowly. "It's scarce loyal to Maister Will. But how can a man tell nowadays what *is* wrong—or what's reight, for that matter?"

16

At the St. Crispen

NOT FAR FROM the parish church of Halifax stood the St. Crispin Inn. Above its entrance, a flickering lantern swung in the wind: the rays from this were too feeble to do more than afford an indistinct glimpse of the shadowy figures that from time to time passed through the door of the inn from the darkness of the street outside.

Once inside, most of the arrivals on this particular evening did not linger in the lighted passages, nor turn towards the warm comfort of the tap or the coffee room. Instead, they moved quickly—almost furtively, thought the landlord uneasily—to a steep staircase at the back of the premises which led to a large upstairs room. At the foot of this staircase, a man loitered who sharply accosted every stranger who went that way: those whom he permitted to pass, encountered two further sentinels at the head of the stairs.

This performance had not escaped the notice of the landlord. Usually a jovial man, ready to share in either a jest or a tankard, tonight his face wore a worried frown. His wife observed it, and quizzed him shrewishly.

"What's amiss, Joe? Tha looks as sick as a cat! 'Tis all that pudden—I've telt thee often enough tha shouldn't stuff thysen when there's work to be done—

for we're reight brisk this evenin', an' no mistake. Anyone'd think it was a Saturday."

"Bain't the pudden," replied Joe, sulkily, "I've been werriting over that lot——" he jerked a thumb upwards—"in t' club room. What're they up to, I'd like to know? There's a chap on t' stair, keepin' folks out, I reckon."

His wife shrugged, and vigorously wiped a cloth over the wet counter. "So long as they buys our ale, reckon it's nowt to do wi' us what they gets up to. Tha'll need to go down to t' cellar just now for more, so look lively, do!"

This sharp injunction recalled the landlord to his duties; and, for the next twenty minutes, he was too occupied to spare a thought to the Democratic Club.

He was reminded of it again when he went into the coffee room to take orders from the customers there. A man and a young woman were standing inconspicuously just inside the door: from habit, he ran a practised eye over them. It was part of a landlord's stock in trade to be able to assess customers at a glance, and this appeared to be an oddly-assorted pair. The man was a respectable-looking workman, most likely of some standing in his own particular line of business, for when he spoke, his voice had the rough authority of one used to handling others. The young lady appeared more gently bred than her companion. Joe thought that she had the look of an impoverished clergyman's daughter, and he noted the strain in her pale face and clouded eyes.

"There's a club meets here," stated the man. "Democratic Club, it calls itself. Canst tak' me to it?"

Mine host sucked in his breath, and shook his head. He was not a quick thinker.

"Ay, there's a club—" he began.

"Which way?" asked Nick Bradley, starting forward.

"Upstairs," replied Joe, slowly. "But tha'll never be takin' t' young lady? Reckon they don't have females—don't know as they'll have thee, think on. They're reight partic'lar."

Bradley looked sharply at him. "Art tryin' to jest, man?"

"Not me." Joe shook his large head from side to side. "Just trying to give thee a friendly word o' advice. But please thysen—it's nowt to do wi' me."

He began to turn away, but the other man put a hand on his arm.

"Wait a bit. Where's this stair, then?"

"If tha cares to come wi' me, I'll show thee. This way."

Bradley turned to Mary. "Wait here, lass, you don't move till I come back."

She cast a frightened glance at the grandfather clock standing against one wall of the room. Already it was a quarter past seven.

"Yes, but hurry up and find him," she replied, in a whisper. "That's if he's here yet—pray Heaven he is!"

He murmured something reassuring, and she nodded, seating herself on a chair close to the door. Bradley turned to follow the landlord down the passage. Halfway along, Joe halted, and pointed to the far end, which was less well-lit than the rest.

"Round to t' left," he directed. "There's a man there, watchin' like."

Bradley continued along the passage, and, turning to the left, saw a steep, dim staircase immediately before him. As he approached it, a figure loomed out of the shadows and stood directly in his path.

"Who's that?" growled a voice.

"Don't matter who I am," replied Nick, shortly. "Is there a lad up there called John Booth? I want a word wi' him."

"Dost tha, now? Well, happen he don't want to talk wi' thee," retorted the other.

"He'll be the best judge o' that, I reckon. Just give him t' message, wilt?"

"I haven't said he's here, yet. Nor won't, till I know who's askin'," was the surly reply.

"Tell him it's his cousin wants him."

"Reckon his cousin's got a name?"

"Ay, but I'm not shoutin' it all over t' place. 'Tis a lass—she's sent me to fetch him to her."

"Petticoats, eh?" The man gave a lewd chuckle.

"Well, reckon she'll 'ave to wait. There'll be plenty o' time for courtin' after t' meeting's finished."

"Nowt o' t' sort," retorted Nick, angrily. " 'Tis an important matter—she must see t' lad at once. Wilt do as I ask, an' tell him?"

"I've not said as he's here."

Nick let loose a ripe oath. "Give over foolin', an' find out—or let me by to do it."

"Let thee by? What dost tak' me for? Who art, that thinks to give orders? Let's have tha name, or by gum——"

Nick made no answer, but pushed past him, and started up the stairs.

He had not gone far when he felt himself seized in a rough grasp by several pairs of hands. Two men had rushed from the top of the stairs to join their companion at the foot.

"What's to do?" they demanded, while Nick Bradley struggled to free himself.

"This chap wants to see someone in t' clubroom. Reckons it's urgent, but won't give his name."

"Let's see his face, then," suggested one of the men. "Happen we'll know him."

"Happen he'll know us, too," muttered another in a warning tone.

"Not likely. Bring him to t' top, lads."

Nick Bradley was a short, tough specimen of manhood, but he could do nothing against three men. Willy-nilly, he was dragged to the head of the stairs, and brought to a halt outside the door of the clubroom. Two of the men held him firmly, while a third stooped, and picked up a dark lantern. He held it before Nick's face, and cautiously slid back the shutter a little way.

Nick turned his head quickly, to try and catch a sight of his captors' faces, but, quick as thought, the man with the lantern covered it again, before the brief glimpse could betray him or his companions. They had all managed to see Nick's face clearly in that brief moment, and one of them exclaimed in satisfaction.

"Ay—I know him reight enough, though I've forgotten his name. He's t' overseer at Liversedge mill."

At this point, Nick began to struggle more violently,

and opened his mouth to shout for assistance; but the call never sounded. One of the men cracked him on the skull with a truncheon that swung from his arm. The overseer sank to the ground, and lay still.

"What'll we do wi' him?" asked one of the men.

"There's a cupboard in t' clubroom," answered another. "Let's shove 'im in there."

"He's not dead, is he?" asked the one who had first spoken.

"Nay—reckon his skull's tougher nor that," was the reply. "He'll come to, presently, but he'll be safer locked up in t' cupboard."

After Nick left her, Mary sat for some time without moving, her eyes fixed anxiously on the door. If John were here already, there could be no reason why Bradley should not return with him in five or ten minutes at the most. Then they could all three be clear of the inn well before the soldiers arrived. She and Nick had discussed this matter thoroughly on the journey into Halifax: they had both agreed that, in all probability, the soldiers would arrive after, rather than before, the time fixed for the meeting. In this way, there would be more chance of catching all the culprits at once.

When the ten minutes had expired which she had judged to be reasonable, she began to fidget. Once, she opened the door, and peered along the passage in the direction Nick had taken; but still he did not appear. His instructions to her to remain there had been explicit, but something might have gone wrong. Why should he not have returned by now? Assuming that John was already in the inn, there had been plenty of time for them to have joined her; while, if John had not yet arrived, Nick's return should have been even more prompt.

She resumed her seat for another few moments, drawing off her gloves and putting them on again with restless movements which spoke of tension. She glanced yet once more at the clock, and saw with a sinking feeling that it was already half past seven.

She jumped up resolutely. Something must be done. She could no longer sit here waiting.

She closed the door of the coffee room behind her, and stood irresolutely in the passage for a moment. She had no clear idea which way Nick had gone, and was hoping to see either the landlord or one of the servants, so that she might inquire.

No one appeared, and she was too conscious of the passage of time to linger there. She knew that the room she wanted was upstairs, so she must first find the staircase. As there was no sign of one where she stood, she walked along the passage in the direction Nick had taken earlier.

At first, she turned to the right; but a very brief walk brought her to a door which opened out into the courtyard of the inn. She saw that she had taken the wrong turning, and, hurriedly retracing her steps, found the staircase she was seeking. There was no one about.

She glanced upward. At the top, a crack of light showed round a door which had been left slightly ajar. This might be the room she wanted.

She caught a quick breath. Without stopping for further thought, she ran swiftly up the stairs, her light, heelless shoes making no sound. Putting her hand on the door, she cautiously edged it open a little more. Then she peered timidly round it.

It was a sparsely furnished and ill-lit room, but at first her eye did not take in all its details. Two things she did notice clearly. One was the knot of men gathered about an open cupboard at the end of the room farthest from her: the other was a tattered screen which had been pulled away from the door, and now stood at the side of it, very close to the wall. She could touch the screen easily with her outstretched hand.

She made up her mind in a moment. Something— she did not know what—was keeping the attention of the occupants of the clubroom focused on the cupboard. She seized her chance, and, slipping round the door, eased herself behind the screen in one swift, lithe movement. Then she leaned out and gently pushed the door back as she had found it, finally moving the side of the screen a little so that it shielded her from the view of anyone using the door.

It all took only a moment, and she was inside the room, safely hidden from a superficial scrutiny. Anyone who approached the screen from its other side might still observe her, for she did not dare to move it again. But there was no one at this end of the room at present; and, with luck, perhaps no one would come close enough to find her out.

She had no clear idea of what she meant to do. Obviously, it would be foolhardy to approach the group boldly, and ask for her cousin. If they were indeed Luddites, they would give her short shrift. She should soon be able to see if he were present among them: if so, she must rely on inspiration to show her a way of giving him her warning.

She was reminded unpleasantly of the night when she had first come to Liversedge. Her knees trembled now as violently as they had done on that occasion, and once again her heart seemed to be beating in her parched mouth—she knew that there was not much time. In half an hour—perhaps more, perhaps less—the soldiers would arrive. By that time, John must be well away from the St. Crispin. This meant that she must issue her warning some time during the next ten minutes. How, she could not foresee.

Up to now, she had been much too occupied with her own thoughts and fears to take in what was happening at the far end of the room. Once safely settled in behind the screen, however, she began to realize that some kind of argument was taking place. At first, the voices were too distant for her to distinguish the words, but, gradually, they grew clearer. At the same time, a heavy clumping of boots told her that the group had moved away from the cupboard, and nearer to her place of concealment.

"I tell thee he's a'raight," said someone, truculently. "He's a thick head on 'im, has Nick Bradley, bad cess to him."

She started violently at mention of Nick's name. What had happened to him? Had these people done him any harm?

"But—but—you don't know how b-badly he's injured—they sh-shouldn't have hit him. And to p-push him in a c-cupboard——"

Although she had expected to find John here, she recognized his voice with dismay. What he had just said sent a cold shiver down her spine: it seemed that they had attacked Nick Bradley, as she had feared. She prayed that he might not be badly hurt, that they might all three come off safely from this terrible adventure. For a moment, in her agony of mind, she lost track of the voices.

When she had gained sufficient control of herself to follow them again, she realized that several of them were arguing with John. There was something they wanted him to do; and he was refusing, though with less and less conviction as each one piled argument on argument. It was difficult to follow the exact words, for they all spoke at once, and most of them shouted. John's voice, too, had developed the high, falsetto tone that it took on in moments of stress. At last, someone shouted for silence, and Mary shuddered involuntarily. She would have recognized that voice anywhere. It was George Mellor's.

"We'll have an end o' it," he pronounced, violently. "Tha knows well enough, John Booth, that t' time for fine talk's past—action's what we need, and what we'll have!" There was a cheer at this. "And so, lad, tha'll need to mak' up tha mind now—this minute." There was a pause. "Art for us—or agin us?" concluded the speaker, ferociously.

There was another cheer. Mary noticed a frayed portion of the screen just below the level of her eyes, and bent her head to it, in order to try and obtain a view of the room beyond. She found that the worn threads offered an imperfect peep-hole which did not allow her to discern the features of the group. It was better than not being able to see at all.

They were standing in a rough circle, with John—she knew him instantly, in spite of the difficulties—in the middle, together with Mellor, whom she soon identified by his voice.

He repeated his question. After a momentary hesitation, John replied.

"You—you know I'm with you, George. But—but——"

"There'll be no buts," said Mellor, roughly. "Tha'lt be twisted in, lad, like t' rest—then there'll be an end o' tha nonsense. Who's got t' Book?"

John began a protest, but he was shouted down, and Mary saw someone thrust a book into his hand. She longed to cry out, but dared not do so, for fear the group might do some harm to her cousin, as well as herself, if she were discovered. How could she stop them, without declaring herself? She racked her brains feverishly to think of a way. And all the time, the hands of the clock were creeping on—it was almost twenty minutes to eight by the one hanging on the wall, above the conspirators' heads.

"Repeat after me," ordered Mellor. " 'I, John Booth——' "

John's voice began the words of the Luddite Oath; stumbling a little every now and then, and tailing away to a whisper after the first few sentences. Mary listened in growing alarm.

"——do solemnly swear that I will never reveal to any person under the canopy of Heaven the names of the persons who compose this Secret Committee, their proceedings, meeting places, places of abode, connections, or anything else that might lead to the discovery of the same, whether by word, deed or sign; under penalty of being sent out of the world by the first brother who shall meet me——"

His voice had now sunk so low that she had to strain every nerve to hear what followed, and kept missing a few words here and there.

"And I further now do swear, that I will use my best endeavours to punish by death any traitor . . . wherever I find him . . . should he fly to the verge of nature, I will pursue . . . So help me, God, and . . . keep my Oath inviolable."

In her anxiety to hear what John was saying, she had been pressing her head closer and closer to the screen. Suddenly it wobbled dangerously, and she put out her hands to try and steady it. Her fingers caught in the frayed patch which she had been using as a peephole. There was an ominous tearing sound; the screen swayed violently for a moment, then fell with a clatter to the floor, sending up a cloud of dust.

All eyes turned towards her. For a moment, no one moved or spoke. Mary stood stricken with terror, surveying the ring of startled faces which showed pale in the yellow light of the tallow dips. Then George Mellor and John Booth together took a step forward.

"What in hell——?" thundered the former.

Mary rushed to John, and flung her arms about him.

"You must go!" she said, breathlessly. "Now—at once! The soldiers are coming to search this place—they'll be here at eight o'clock, or soon after——"

"M-Mary! What—what are you doing——?"

"What's that tha's sayin'?" asked Mellor, pulling her roughly away from her cousin. "S'ojers? What's that about Redcoats?"

He thrust his face close to hers, and the nightmare quality of the man almost made her scream aloud. She tried to pull herself free, but he only tightened his grasp so that his strong fingers dug relentlessly into her flesh.

"It's true," she gasped. "They're coming—someone gave word of this meeting——" she turned her head towards John, straining away from Mellor with all her frantic strength—"Oh, go now, I beg of you—else it will be too late!"

John seized Mellor's arm urgently. "L-let her go—you must let her go, George! You're hurting her!"

"Nowt to what I'll do to her, if she's playin' off tricks," growled Mellor. "Is this true, tha baggage?"

"Oh, go, John, go!" she insisted, almost sobbing in her anxiety to convince him of his danger. "They know the meeting is for eight o'clock—they'll arrive then, or soon after—for the love of Heaven, go quickly!"

"By gum, I reckon it's reight," said Mellor, releasing her abruptly, so that she almost fell. "Ye know what to do, lads—we've bin through all this afore—we'll meet on t' Moor, as planned—get out, quick!"

There was a general exodus. Mellor grabbed John's arm.

"Come on, lad, look lively! I know where we'll be safe enough till they've gone!"

John shook him off. "Mary—I can't leave you——"

"You must, you must! For your father's sake—and mine, John! Go with—that man. I'll be all right. Nick brought me here——" She stopped all at once recollecting what had happened to Nick Bradley.

"Nick? They—they've——" began John.

"Come on, lad, for God's sake!" Mellor pulled him headlong in the direction of the door. He turned briefly to throw a word to Mary. "Tha'll find Bradley in t' cupboard. He'll be none t' worse, I reckon, by now. Don't fret ower tha cousin—I'll tak' care o' him, reight enough. Don't look to see 'im back 'ome for a day or two."

She nodded, scarcely knowing what she did, and watched while Mellor propelled John through the door. She noticed that though he handled her cousin firmly, he was not unduly rough with him; and she thought with surprise that the black giant seemed always to have a kind of rough concern for this young man whom he might well have despised.

After they had gone, she stood still for a moment, trying to recover from the exhausting emotions of the last hour. Then she roused herself, and went over to the cupboard.

She half feared to look inside; but, conquering the feeling, turned the key and opened the door.

Nick Bradley was sitting up in a slouched attitude, a slightly bemused look on his face. She bent over him with relief.

"Oh, thank Heavens! Are you all right?"

"Ay—reight enough," he said, struggling to his feet.

She put out an arm to help him. "Can you manage? Or shall I get the landlord?"

"Nay." He had managed to stand erect, and now moved unsteadily forward into the room. "Reckon I'll be a'reight in a little while."

"Do you think you could walk downstairs?" she asked anxiously. "Or do you need help from someone stronger than myself? I don't think we should remain here—the soldiers might ask us awkward questions."

"By gum, ay—I'd forgot that." He passed a hand across his brow, and winced slightly. "What time is it? Did young John get away? Or wasn't he here?"

"He's safe," she answered, shortly. There would be time later to go into that. "But we must leave here without delay. If you can manage to reach the place where we left the gig, I can drive us home."

"I'll manage, lass."

"Then take my arm. I've found a door just beyond the foot of the staircase which leads directly into the courtyard. It's quiet and dark there, we should be able to leave unobserved."

Reluctantly, he did as she asked, and together they slowly descended the staircase. They met no one on their journey to the courtyard and it was not long before they reached the gig.

Mary helped her companion to ascend, then untethered the horse, and herself climbed up into the vehicle.

"I'll not light the lamp, yet," she whispered as she drew the rug around Nick.

She took up the reins, competently guiding the light vehicle on to the road which led to Liversedge.

They had gone only a short distance, when they heard the bell on the parish church clock telling the hour.

Five minutes later, from the distance came the sound of galloping hoofs and the jingle of harness, as the military rode on a fruitless errand to the St. Crispin Inn.

17

A Visitor for Mary

MARY AWOKE NEXT morning with a heavy depression of spirits. She was so quiet over breakfast that her uncle became solicitous, asking if she would not have done better to rest in bed for the day. Although this kindness made her feel guilty, it did at least offer her a further respite from the necessity of confessing the truth about her absence from Mr. Arkwright's house. She knew that this must be faced soon; but at present, while her anxieties over John were so pressing, she did not feel equal to it. She told herself that tomorrow, come what may, her uncle must know what had really happened.

After breakfast, she asked Mrs. Duckworth to find her something to do, and finally settled down in the parlour with a pile of mending. There was a letter to be written home, but she was in no mood for that, knowing her mother's ability to read between the lines. Mrs. Lister would sense that all was not well with her daughter; when so many miles divided them, it would be cruel to rouse her anxiety. Moreover, it might not be long before they were reunited, when Mary could tell her own story.

She applied herself industriously to the task of replacing buttons and darning hose, and even managed to achieve a degree of tranquillity after a time. There was a soothing quality about the quiet, domestic task, after the dramatic happenings of the past few days. Vaguely, she heard a knock sound on the Vicarage door, and Mrs. Duckworth's hurried step in the passage outside, as she went to answer it. Even when the parlour door opened, and Mrs. Duckworth poked her head round it, Mary was still only half aware of the interruption.

The next moment, she was immediately plunged into a state of extreme awareness and confusion.

"Mr. Arkwright to see you, Miss Mary."

She started up from her chair, a torn shirt of her uncle's clutched in her hand. Her face paled a little, then gradually was suffused by a faint blush.

"I—I can't see him——" she began weakly.

It was too late, for Mr. Arkwright strode into the room, nodding to the housekeeper to close the door. She did so, and left them alone.

He gave Mary a brusque good morning, and then seemed at a loss how to continue. She could not help him, and for a few moments they stood silently facing each other, waiting to see who would begin.

At last she could not bear the silence any longer, and uttered the first words that came into her head.

"I—perhaps you wished to see my uncle?"

"No. It was you I came to see."

"Oh—well——" she stammered. "I—I thought that everything had been said between us that there was to say."

"Not quite." His tone was still curt; and, now that she was recovering a little from her first embarrassment at seeing him, she found herself resenting this. "There is something still to say—or to retract, rather."

"I don't understand."

"No? Well, it's not the easiest thing in the world to explain. The fact is——" he hesitated, then went on quickly—"I fear that I may have been a little hasty, yesterday."

She made no reply, but looked at him expectantly.

"You must admit," he said, abruptly, "that appearances were against you. The letter—found in your pocket, so you said——"

"It happens to be true," she replied, coldly.

"Perhaps: but——"

"There is no 'perhaps' or 'but' about it," said Mary, indignantly. "I don't propose to go through a repetition of the scene we had yesterday. So if that is all you have to say to me, Mr. Arkwright, you had better leave."

"Listen to me, woman," he commanded, "and don't be such a firebrand. I was only——"

"A firebrand? I?" She threw up her head, and a dangerous spark came into her eyes. "And what do you think you are, pray?"

"I'll admit that I am no sucking dove," he said, with a dry smile.

"That you are not!" she retorted. She had nothing to lose now, and the repressed indignation of several weeks was burning on her tongue. "I don't know when I have ever met such a quick-tempered, autocratic, unreasonable——"

"That will do," he said, sharply.

"I am not obliged to take your orders now," she pointed out. "I am free to speak my own mind."

He stared at her. "Evidently I have been deceived in you," he said, in a stern tone. "I thought you a gentle, prettily-behaved female——"

"Did you also think me entirely devoid of spirit?" asked Mary. "Did you think you could insult me, and I would say nothing? Words are a woman's only weapon—you must expect her to use it."

"I know this much," he said, taking a step towards her. "If you were my sister, I should lay you across my knee, young woman."

"How dare you!" An angry flush stained her cheek, and she stepped back hastily, for fear he should think of putting his threat into execution.

"Oh, for pity's sake!" he exclaimed, with an impatient gesture. "Why the devil do I always seem to be at loggerheads with you? I didn't think myself so completely lacking in address—and you have tact and charm enough, when you choose to exercise them——"

"I will not listen," said Mary, with compressed lips, "to any more of your insults! I will ask Mrs. Duckworth to show you out."

She threw the garment she was still clutching down on the table, and moved towards the door. He caught her by the arm.

"Confound it, no—not yet! I haven't told you what I came here to say."

"Kindly release me," she said, coldly.

"Damned if I will," he retorted, taking both her arms in his grasp, and swinging her round to face him. "Now you listen to me, young woman——"

Afterwards, she was to wonder why she should have behaved as she did. Mr. Arkwright seemed to have the trick of stirring strange emotions within her.

She tore one arm free from his grasp, and, before he could make a move to recover it, dealt him a stinging slap on the face.

"You—you hell cat!" he said, between clenched teeth.

For a moment, she feared that he was about to retaliate in kind, and flinched away from him. But he did not strike her; instead, he crushed her to him in a fierce grip that seemed as though it would break every bone in her body. Then he tilted her chin roughly upwards, and pressed his mouth ruthlessly on hers.

He held her there for what seemed an interminable time: then he released her so abruptly that she staggered, and had to clutch at the table for support.

"Oh!" she gasped, and covered her face with her hands.

He surveyed her with grim satisfaction. "Yes," he said. "I thought you would dislike that. Let it be a lesson to you not to play off hoydenish tricks."

She raised her burning face, and looked at him with angry eyes.

"How dare you! How dare you treat me like a—like a——"

"Oh, but I didn't, I assure you," he said, with a sardonic smile. "Not if we are thinking of the same word, that is."

"I won't listen to such—such improper talk—and under my uncle's roof, too!" she stormed.

"Well, you began it, my dear," he replied, still smiling. "Tell me, do you consider it proper to indulge in fisticuffs with visitors under your uncle's roof, as you put it?"

"You deserved that," she retorted," and I am glad—yes, glad—that I did it, however unladylike it may have been!"

"No doubt. And I am just as glad, believe me——" his dark eyes mocked her—"that I retaliated as I did."

"Oh!" She turned away in confusion.

"But I won't tease you," he continued, good-humouredly. "I came here on a peaceful errand, you know, not to pick a quarrel. I have been thinking over what I said to you yesterday, and it seems less than fair." He paused. "I am prepared to accept your account concerning the letter."

"That is very good of you," she said, tartly.

"Yes, well, under the circumstances, I think it is," he replied, coolly. "Consider the facts—I've known you for a very short time, your cousin had Luddite sympathies. I'm not in a position to be able to take anyone on trust. In making an exception of you, I'm going against reason—as you must acknowledge, if you're to weigh the matter objectively."

"I am not in an objective frame of mind, at present, Mr. Arkwright."

"So I have observed. But come, now, accept my apology, there's a good girl, and let's consider the business at an end."

"Apology? You call that an apology?"

"Why not? I've acknowledged that I was hasty."

"Without," Mary reminded him, "asking my pardon for it."

"What do you want me to do?" he asked, a shade testily. "Go on my knees to you?"

"No. But I think you might show some contrition for the——" she faltered "—for the upset you have caused."

"Very well, then, I do ask your pardon. There, are you satisfied now?"

She shook her head. "No, Mr. Arkwright, I am not. From your tone, I collect that you think it a small thing to lose your temper with those who cannot answer you back—and when you choose to receive them into favour again, they must be ready and willing to forgive you at once, without ceremony."

"Why not? Those who know me well, know also that I mean nothing by it. My bark is worse than my bite, as I think I told you before this." He shrugged. "We all have faults—this is one of mine, if you will."

"And you don't mean to do anything to cure it," said Mary, mockingly. "Most of us try to overcome our faults—you seem almost proud of yours."

He looked at her for a moment without replying.

"Be careful, ma'am," he warned, at last. "Do not drive me too far, or I may be obliged to repeat my performance of a few moments since."

The colour once more flooded her cheeks.

"How you *can* remind me——" she began, in a muffled voice.

"Do I need to?" His dark eyes deepened momentarily. "For myself, I shan't find it easy to forget."

"You—I——" she faltered, her eyes dropping before his intent look. "You have no right to say such things," she resumed, more spiritedly. "I don't care for gallantry, sir."

"That depends, does it not?" There was an edge to his light tone. "On who is offering it to you, I mean."

"I see you are determined to insult me," said Mary, with dignity. "You'd best go, Mr. Arkwright. I accept your apology—such as it is——"

He started to speak, then evidently thought better of it, standing for a moment in silence.

"Very well," he said, at last. "I'll see you tomorrow, then?"

It was more of a statement than a question. She stared in surprise.

"See me—tomorrow?"

He nodded. "Yes—you feel equal to it, I imagine? If you would like a few more days at home, I am perfectly willing——"

"Do I understand you aright, sir? You are asking me to return to your employ?"

"Of course—what else?"

"But—after all that has passed——"

"My dear Miss Lister," he said, formally, "it is a great mistake to refine too much upon the past. I made a mistake—I have apologized—you have accepted my apology. There is no reason that I can see why everything cannot be just as it was before."

Again she stared at him. "No, I believe you really can't," she said, incredulously. "All that has happened, both yesterday and—and——" she faltered a moment —"now, today—it all means nothing to you. It might never have been."

"That's not quite true." He gave her a deep, intent look that made her turn away quickly. "There is one thing I shall remember, at any rate. But, for the rest— whatever hard things we may have said to each other, I shall not think of them again."

"You are fortunate in having such an accommodating memory," she said; but she did not look at him.

"I found out early in life that there's no profit in thinking of disagreeable things. Write off your bad memories as you write off your bad debts, and show a clean sheet. It's the only way."

She shook her head. "I can't aspire to it."

"Come, ma'am, I should have said you were a for-giving person."

"Yes—but not one who forgets entirely."

"Well, try to forget. I assure you, I shall not think of any of this—save one thing, as I said before." He paused, waiting for her to answer, but she was silent. "Shall I see you tomorrow? Or is that too soon?"

"No, Mr. Arkwright." She faced him resolutely. "You will not see me tomorrow—or at any time, in your house as your sister's governess."

He stared at her incredulously. "You do not mean to return?"

"No. It would not do. I must look for a post else-where—nearer my own home, I think."

"May I ask why it would not do?"

She hesitated. The reasons which came first to mind were not those she wished to voice.

"Is it anything," he persisted, "to do with what has happened here today? If so, I promise you—though re-luctantly—that it will not occur again. While you are in my house, you need have nothing to fear—from me, or from anyone else."

"No—it's not only that—I—oh, it would not an-swer!"

"Perhaps you do not believe I should keep my promise?"

Her eyes refused to meet his.

"It's not that—but after all that's occurred—things can never be quite the same, I should not be comfort-able any more."

"But you are no bread-and-butter miss, to be frightened off by a brush with reality——"

"A governess is always in a difficult situation, Mr. Arkwright. She is neither a servant, nor yet one of the family. If a proper distance cannot be maintained——"

"A proper distance!" The words were scornful, but there was a gentler expression in his eyes. "I suspect that the proper distance between us is——"

He broke off, seeming suddenly to recollect himself.

"Caroline wants you back," he continued, in a dif-ferent tone. "I told her you were indisposed, and would return in a day or two. You have won her affection, you know—she would miss you sadly."

"Was that why you came?" asked Mary, involuntarily. "Because Caroline wants me to return, and has been urging you to come and see me?"

"No." He took a step towards her and she could see that he was in the grip of a strong emotion. "Caroline misses you, certainly—so do I."

She drew a quick breath, and turned towards the table, seizing a garment from the pile of mending as though she meant to resume her interrupted task. She had no very clear idea at that moment of what she was doing.

"It's no use," she said, breathlessly. "I am sorry—I, too, am fond of your sister, but I know it will never be the same again. And besides, perhaps in time I might do something else to vex you, and then you would ask me to go a second time. As you said yourself, we seem to be always at loggerheads, you and I. It will be better if I go now."

She was staring from the window as she spoke: it looked out to the front of the Vicarage. As she watched, a figure entered the gate, and began to walk up the path towards the door.

"I fancy I know why we quarrel so easily," Arkwright said, softly. "Shall I tell you, I wonder?"

"There—there is someone coming to the house," she said, hurriedly, to hide her confusion.

"Let him be damned, whoever he is," he retorted, impatiently. "Miss Lister—Mary lass——"

"I believe it is Mr. Webster," she continued, her thoughts in a riot.

He moved to her side. "Will you listen? I——" He broke off. His eyes followed the direction of hers, and alighted on the man who was now close to the house.

"Arthur Webster!" he exclaimed, in a different tone. "So you were expecting him! Now I see why you don't wish to return to my house."

She turned a startled face towards him as the knocker sounded.

"But I had no idea——" she began.

"No?" He gave a short, hard laugh, and moved

towards the door. "Well, I will not intrude upon your tête-à-tête. No doubt you now have other plans for your future than those which had begun to occur to me."

He reached the door, and made her an ironic bow.

"Don't bother to see me out. I'll go through the back way." He paused. "And I must thank you—I almost made a fool of myself, but you prevented me in time."

18

The Defence of the Mill

ARKWRIGHT COVERED THE short distance between the Vicarage and his own house in record time. Glancing at his face as she admitted him, Nellie shivered, and searched her memory in quick panic for any misdeed which could possibly be laid at her door. The fact that she could not think of anything failed to relieve her strong feelings of guilt. Something had put the Master about sadly; and, if she knew the signs, someone would pay for it.

Caroline had heard his knock, and came limping out of the parlour, closing the door carefully behind her. The injured ankle was almost normal again, but it still would not hurry along as its owner's usual headlong pace.

"Did you see her, Will?" she asked, in a low, eager voice. "Can she return soon—tomorrow, or the next day?"

"I saw her," he said, grimly. "She will not return at all."

Caroline gave a cry. "Not come back here? Not at all? Oh, why not? Is she seriously ill?"

He shook his head. "She does not choose to come."

She limped forward, and clutched his arm. "Why

not? She must have a reason——Will, you haven't been vexed with her, and——and said something to frighten her away——"

He shook off her arm irritably. "I want to hear no more of Miss Lister from now on——do you understand? No more."

She looked as if she would protest, but thought better of it; then her lip began to tremble ominously.

He drew her roughly to him for a moment. "Oh, for God's sake, child——you're not the only one who will miss her! But it's best so, believe me. And now, no more of this. Where's your Mama?"

Caroline pointed to the parlour. "In there," she said, gulping a little. "And——and Colonel Grey is waiting to see you——he came a short while back."

He released her, and strode into the parlour, to find his stepmother giving an uneasy audience to the Colonel. She looked up in palpable relief at his entrance.

"Oh, I'm so glad you're come, Will, for the Colonel wanted particularly to see you, and says he has not much time to spare." She rose, nervously gathering up her embroidery materials and her reticule in hands which failed to retain most of the objects in their grasp. "I'll leave you alone——"

"No need for that," replied Arkwright, stooping to retrieve a pair of scissors and a skein of silk from the carpet. "We'll go into the library, by your leave, sir."

The Colonel assented, and the two men left Mrs. Arkwright to the healing effects of solitude.

"Last night's affair was a fiasco," said the Colonel, when they were settled. "The men turned out for nothing."

Arkwright's eyebrows shot up. "No meeting?" he asked. "I thought that spy was a fool, but not such a fool as that."

"Undoubtedly there was a meeting," replied Colonel Grey. "My men questioned the landlord pretty closely, and he admitted to feeling uneasy about a watch that was being kept on the stairs which led to the Club room. He also said that most of the men seemed to have arrived by just after seven, though he denied knowing any of 'em, or even paying any particular attention to their activities. Was busy in the tap and the cellar, so he said." Arkwright nodded. "The thing is, when my fellows arrived, it was too late. They left it until just on the hour, so's not to scare any of the birds off—when they got there, the lot had flown. A few traces of 'em in the room itself, and the landlord's evidence—but not a single man there to be taken."

"Warned, do you suppose?" asked the mill-owner, wrinkling his forehead. "But by whom?"

Colonel Grey shrugged. "Possibly. Or they may have started the meeting early, as most members had arrived by seven, according to the landlord. Perhaps an hour was sufficient for their purposes."

"I don't like it," demurred Arkwright. "It looks like treachery. But who would know?"

"The soldiers, of course," replied the Colonel, thoughtfully. "As far as I know, they're to be trusted—they're all Regulars. It's possible someone might have overheard them talking about the raid. I told no one else—I don't know about you?"

"No one," answered Arkwright, promptly. "At least——" he hesitated—"no one who could possibly betray me. My overseer, Nick Bradley, knew about it."

"You're sure of him?"

"As sure as I am of myself. He served my father, and helped me put the business on its legs again after his death. No—not Nick, decidedly not."

"As you say. Well, it doesn't greatly matter now, does it? The thing is, we know that a meeting was held, and all the evidence seems to suggest it was a meeting of the Luddites. Plans were made there, for certain; and, in view of the threatening letter you received, it's any odds you care to mention that those plans concerned an early attack on your mill."

Arkwright nodded. "I'm sure of it, too. In all cases, a threatening letter has been quickly followed by an attack. I'd say, myself, they'd make the attempt within the next few days."

"You sound cool enough," approved the Colonel. "Have you made any plans for defending your property?"

Arkwright nodded. "I've been working on them ever since I first decided to bring machines into the mill. I'll explain, sir. I propose to defend the place from the upper floor—it's paved with stone flags, and I've fitted rings and pulleys on to them, so that they can be raised in order to fire on anyone who succeeds in entering the ground floor. It will also be possible from there to fire obliquely through the windows, so that we can command the front of the mill. I shall confine all invaders to the ground floor by the expedient of my own patent device."

He drew a sheet of paper towards him, and, picking up a pen from the inkstand, drew a rough sketch of a large roller with vicious-looking spikes protruding from it.

"I shall fit these contraptions to the stairs," he explained. "Anyone who succeeds in surmounting them—and I don't think it likely, as these spikes are eighteen inches long—will find a huge carboy of vitriol waiting for him at the top of the stairs. The threat of this should be sufficient"——his face took on grim lines—"but if they persist, they'll get it, right enough."

"That's the spirit!" approved the Colonel. "Your place will be as well defended as a mediaeval fortress—and on much the same lines. Now—what about men?"

"Two watchmen armed with blunderbusses at the gates, to give warning," enumerated Arkwright. "Three or four completely reliable workmen, four or five of the best men in my Volunteers, and myself. That's the muster, sir."

"But you'll need the Army," protested Colonel Grey. "Now's our chance to smoke out this nest of Luddites, and it'll not be done by a handful of labourers and toy soldiers, believe me! They may come in their hundreds, by all we've heard."

Arkwright shook his head. "We can't have a force of any size hidden away in the mill," he objected. "Moreover, the Ludds will only attack if they believe the place to be practically unguarded. Any suspicion of the military in the vicinity, and they'll be frightened off, you may depend. They haven't yet reached the stage of declaring open warfare on the Army."

"There's much in what you say." The Colonel nodded thoughtfully. "But this is too good a chance to miss, for all that—we must make sure of capturing the ringleaders, at least, as I'd hoped to do last night at the St. Crispin." He paused. "Tell you what then," he continued. "You keep to your original plans for the defence of your property; and I'll billet men at all the inns in the area—say, within a radius of two or three miles of the mill. They'll have orders to keep as close as possible during the daylight hours, and be on the alert after dark every night. All that's needed now is some system of alarm for you to sound off when the attack begins—something that will carry the necessary distance."

"That's simple," Arkwright stated, with satisfaction. "There's a great bell on the roof of the mill—it's not been used for some years, but I'll look it over in readiness. On the still night air, its peal should carry for miles. My watchmen will give us the first alarm; if they fail, there's a large hound patrolling the premises. They'll find it difficult enough to break into the ground floor—those doors are stout, and studded with iron nails. The windows are a weakness; but we shall reinforce them, and, in any case, they would only admit one man at a time. I promise you, Colonel, if they do get in, we shall massacre them—without the aid of the military."

"I believe you will." Colonel Grey glanced approvingly at the grim, determined face of the man beside him. "I say again, Arkwright, what I said before—you're a great loss to the Army, damned if you're not."

He was to repeat this sentiment a couple of nights later, when he arrived unexpectedly at the mill after daylight had faded. He was unaccompanied, and watched appraisingly while Arkwright and his small force of men went round the building making their arrangements. Each evening since Arkwright's last meeting with the Colonel, everything in Liversedge mill had been set in readiness for an attack: each morning, after a sleepless, but uneventful night, the watchers had been obliged to put the place in order again for a normal day's work.

"I'm beginning to feel it's a waste of time," said Arkwright, in return to the Colonel's congratulatory words.

"Then I've news that will change your opinion," said Colonel Grey. "Reports have been coming in steadily of thefts of arms—some large, some small—taken from places within a ten-miles' radius of here. If that don't suggest an attack. I'm a Dutchman. Moreover, the biggest of these thefts took place a few hours since, not far from Huddersfield."

Arkwright raised his brows. "It certainly sounds more hopeful. To tell the truth, I'd be disappointed, now, if they didn't have a crack at us. I feel confident of the outcome, and I'd dearly love to teach them a lesson."

"Can you find me a shake-down for the night?"

"D' you mean to stay, sir?"

"I'd like to, if you'll have me. Call it an old soldier's instinct, if you like, but I've a strong notion that they'll attack tonight."

A chill wind blew over the bleak moor, bending the few stunted trees and tossing the heather. The waiting men shivered, straining their eyes through the darkness in the direction from whence they hoped to see others come marching to join them. Already they were over a hundred strong, desperate men for the most part, eagerly grasping their oddly assorted weapons. In spite of the recent raids, not all carried firearms; some held heavy hammers that had become the trademark of the Luddites, while others had to be content with farm-implements, stakes, or even an improvised cudgel.

There were those among them who secretly wished themselves elsewhere. As they answered the roll-call, they shivered, knowing that now they were irrevocably committed to deeds of which they doubted the justice and feared the outcome. But they knew they dared not retract: they had taken an oath which bound them indissolubly to the Luddite cause, whatever action its leaders might dictate. To turn traitor was to invite an

ignominous death. However little stomach they had for
the present proceedings, they kept silent.

John Booth was one of these. He stood next to Sam
Hartley, his face pale in the moonlight. Most of the
Luddites had either blackened their faces or put on
masks; but these two had shunned the feeble attempt
at concealment. Both were past caring, though for different reasons.

Somewhere a curlew raised its high, plaintive cry.
John shuddered, and hunched his shoulders, as though
attempting to shrink into himself. He started as a heavy
hand clapped him on the shoulder.

"Cold, lad? Tha'll be warm enough just now, when
t' fun starts."

It was Black George, doing the rounds with one or
two others who had placed themselves in command of
the rioters.

"Ay, that we will," Sam Hartley answered him, his
eyes blazing fanatically in his white face. "I've waited
long enough for this day, b'God, and now I'll be even
wi' Arkwright, if it's t' last thing I do in this world—
damn his soul!"

There was a growl of assent from those nearest him.
Booth flinched, but said nothing: his companion's
fierce hate terrified him.

"Tha's reight," approved Mellor, shortly. "Reckon
we've all waited long enough. Well, lads, we'd best be
on our way."

One of the other leaders spoke up. "There's t' lads
from Leeds to come yet," he protested. "Happen
they've been delayed. Let's wait a bit."

"We've waited all we're going to wait," retorted
Mellor firmly. "We need to strike while t' iron's hot—t'
lads'll lose their nerve, I reckon, if we hang about
much longer."

The other demurred, but Black George's forceful-
ness overcame all objections, and the party eventually
moved off across the moor in the direction of Liversedge.

Arkwright and the Colonel had kept up a desultory
conversation until close on midnight, squatting side by

side on the straw paliasses which had been placed for
them on the upper floor of the mill. Most of the other
men on guard were already asleep, worn out by the extra hours of vigil in addition to their normal working
day. At five to twelve, the Colonel looked at his watch,
yawned widely, and stretched his full length on the
mattress.

"Looks as though I was wrong," he said, between
yawns. "They're not coming tonight after all."

He relapsed into silence, closing his eyes. Presently,
a faint snore issued from his lips.

Arkwright leaned back on one elbow, and let his
glance travel once more round the dimly lit room, as
he had done countless times already during the hours
of waiting. He no longer saw it: in his mind's eye was
the Vicarage parlour, with Mary Lister standing there,
as she had confronted him on his last visit. Could it
really have been only a few days since? He seemed to
have lived a lifetime since then; and yet he could still
feel her nearness in his every nerve, when he conjured
up once more the moment when he had held her in his
arms. He told himself that it was no use to think of
that. She had shown him plainly enough where her interest lay; and he was not a sickly youth, to go wailing
for the moon. He had done well enough before Mary
Lister came to Liversedge, and he would do well again,
after she left. All things are passing. And if the ghost
of his younger self suddenly cried out against this staid
philosophy, he knew how to quell it.

Suddenly he started up, every sense alert to the
present emergency. His quick ears had caught the low
growl of the dog from downstairs. He put out a hand,
and shook the Colonel.

"Someone's there," he whispered.

Several of the others had heard the growl, and were
quietly rousing their fellows. In a moment, every man
was on his feet and listening intently.

The dog growled again, tentatively, then more
strongly. They listened, and could hear the muffled
sound of many feet approaching from the distance. The
sound steadily grew in volume as it drew closer to the

mill: then suddenly it stopped, as though cut off with a knife.

The dog now began to bark unrestrainedly. The next moment, there came a sharp, splintering sound, a wild cry of triumph, and a rush of feet into the forecourt of the mill.

"They've broken through the outer gates," stated Arkwright. "Right lads, raise the flagstones."

"Look to your muskets," ordered the Colonel, as soon as the first command was obeyed. "Hold your fire until the word is given."

The men took up their positions as previously arranged, and waited with their firearms at the ready.

Another loud shout rang out, and a shower of stones hailed against the ground floor windows, followed by the crashing sound of breaking glass.

"Not yet," warned Arkwright. "Wait till they close in a bit."

"What's happened to your two watchmen?" asked the Colonel, in a low tone. "Didn't hear them fire, did you?"

"No. Overpowered by now, I expect. Unless they ratted—I chose those I was most sure of for this part of the business." He indicated the interior of the mill with a jerk of his head.

At that moment, there was a wild burst of firing through the shattered downstairs windows. Evidently the rioters had moved in closer to the mill, and were preparing to attempt an entry.

"Now!" ordered Arkwright, sharply. "Fire!"

Those who were stationed at the previously manufactured loopholes along the front of the building let loose a volley of musketry. Its echoes resounded through the quiet valley; for all at once a shocked silence had fallen, as the rioters realized for the first time that the mill was being ably defended by armed men. They had hoped and expected that, as in other places, they would find here only a few inexpert guards with a pistol or so among them, and small science in handling weapons.

A shout from Black George rallied them. A sharp word of command, and they leapt at the great door of the building, their hatchet blades glinting evilly in the moonlight. Simultaneously, another group of them let fly with a bombardment of stones, this time at the upstairs windows where lurked the hidden marksmen. Some missed their mark, for these windows were smaller than those downstairs; but the sound of crashing glass testified to the accuracy of aim of the rest.

Several of the defenders leapt smartly back as flying fragments of glass came their way. One or two suffered minor cuts, but no one was seriously hurt.

"Back to your positions!" ordered the Colonel, momentarily forgetting this was Arkwright's affair.

The men responded, moving forward through jagged heaps of glass fragments which crunched beneath their feet.

"Fire!"

Once again a volley rang through the night. This time, it was followed by groans, and the soft thud of falling bodies.

"Hit a few of 'em," said the Colonel, in satisfaction. "Someone ring that alarm bell, quick! We'll get the military here."

The bell-rope was hanging just beyond the head of the stairs. Arkwright signalled to a workman who was standing guard there; he went over, and seized the rope.

The bell rang out, its urgent clangour echoing high above the noise of the hatchets which struck in vain at the unyielding door. For a moment, the Luddites paused, dismayed at the sound.

"Hammers!" roared Black George. "Use t' hammers—hatchet blades are turning—give way to t' lads wi' hammers!"

The hatchet men fell back, and those armed with hammers took their places. Sparks flew out as time and again they brought down the weapons with their full weight behind them: but still the great door stood firm.

"Side door," whispered one of the leaders, hoarsely. "Door to t' counting house—let's try that."

"Ay—some of ye go there—t' rest keep on here," ordered Mellor.

Those indicated detached themselves, and made

their way cautiously past the counting house to the door in the side of the building. It was no less sturdy than the main door; but it was smaller, and their hopes rose as they began to attack it with vigour.

A heavy burst of firing rained down on them from the windows above. Several of them dropped in their tracks; the rest were forced to abandon the attempt.

"Let's try t' rear," suggested one man, as quietly as he could, for the uproar now was tumultuous. "They're mostly firing on t' front, I reckon—happen we'll find a way in there."

The idea caught on, and the remaining members of the small party crept stealthily to the rear of the building. And now they were thankful for the wild clangour of the alarm bell, and the ring of their comrades' hammers on the great door.

Perhaps a dozen of them reached the rear of the building unnoticed. The windows here were undamaged, and now came the difficult part of their business. They must smash the windows in order to gain admittance, and there was a risk that even in all this din, the noise of breaking glass might draw down fire upon their heads. Yet another difficulty was the fact that the mill had been constructed close to the edge of the river. An incautious step in the dark would send a man plunging headlong into the fast-flowing waters. Several of them now clung precariously to jutting stones, and seemed uncertain of what to do next.

"Try to climb on t' wheel," urged their leader. "We might be able to reach t' small window to t' side of it."

Two or three edged along the bank, eager to make the attempt. Eventually, one did succeed in climbing on to the wheel; but he could not keep his footing on the wet, slimy surface. He slipped, his hands clawed desperately for support, and the next moment a shriek sounded from him as he went hurtling through the air into the waters beneath.

At once, a burst of firing from above spattered around the rest. One or two dropped silently to join their companion in the water; the rest hung for a moment close in to the building, then gradually made their way back to join their comrades in the assault on the main door.

The rioters were growing desperate by now, as the minutes sped by, and still they could not gain an entrance to the building. And the bell kept ever clanging, clanging, calling loudly for assistance.

"Stop that damned bell!" shouted Mellor. "Fire, lads, an' break t' bloody thing!"

Several shots rang out in response to his order, but still the bell continued its strident appeal.

Frantically, Mellor snatched a musket from the man nearest him.

"Shoot, I say! We'll have t' sojers on us, else! Shoot!"

Yet another round of the precious ammunition was expended, but this time to some purpose. The great bell quivered, then fell silent.

A cheer went up. Inside the mill, the defenders looked at each other for a moment in dismay. The bell-rope had slithered uselessly to the floor.

"A lucky shot," said Arkwright. "They've broken the rope." He turned to the Colonel. "Take over here, sir; I'll see what I can do to get it going again."

He signalled to one of the men to accompany him; and, grasping their muskets, they ascended a ladder to a trap-door in the roof. They opened this, and cautiously wriggled out beside the structure which held the bell. A brief survey revealed that the broken rope was swinging within grasp.

"We'll take it in turns to pull," directed Arkwright. "You start. I'll pick some of 'em off, meanwhile, if they look like firing again."

The man was about to obey; but suddenly a loud, splintering crack was heard, and a roar arose from the Luddites.

"T' door's bursted! We've done it—Sam's done it— Sam Hartley! Sam Hartley!"

The name echoed and re-echoed through the throng.

In truth, there was little enough to shout about: the hole they had succeeded in making was little bigger than a man's head, and would need much more work on it before it would admit them, even singly.

"Fire through the hole!" ordered Colonel Grey, sharply, to the two men in the best position for doing so. "Give 'em another volley, the rest of you!"

But one of the two men threw down his musket without a word, and folded his arms.

"D'ye hear!" roared the Colonel. "Fire through that hole in the door!"

The others obeyed at once but the first man still stood motionless.

"Insubordination!" snapped the Colonel. "When this is over, you're under arrest!"

Shrieks and groans rose up from the rioters, giving witness to the accurate aim of the defenders.

"Sam's hit!" arose a shout. "They got him—Sam's hit!"

The man who had thrown down his musket turned fiercely on the Colonel, his eyes blazing in a dead-white face.

"My brother!" he exclaimed, in a choking voice. "God damn thy soul, tha asked me to fire on my own brother—and now he's dead!"

He broke down. Just them, the bell resumed its insistent clamour.

The shot had not killed Sam outright, though he was badly hit. John Booth was close by as he fell, and bent over the still form.

"Sam!" He held his hand for a moment over the other man's heart, and felt the stir of life. "Thank God—oh, thank God!"

He straightened up with the idea of trying to move Hartley away from the thick of the turmoil. As he did so, another fierce volley from above raked the mob.

John Booth dropped beside his companion, shot through the leg.

By now, the Luddite leaders were beginning to suffer from strong misgivings. In spite of their initial success in breaking down a small portion of the door, they found they could make no more headway with it. The defenders were in an impregnable position, under cover, and seemingly, with an inexhaustible supply of ammunition: the Luddites' own scanty stocks were almost finished. Moreover, they had been at the attack for more than half an hour; and, during most of that time, the bell on the roof had never stopped its wild call for help. By now, it must have been heard: before long, they could expect to see the military come charging down upon them.

The disaffection spread rapidly through the ranks: a further barrage of fire from above settled the matter. Cursing vehemently, Black George reluctantly agreed to abandon the attack. All realized the need for haste. They must be miles away from that spot, and safely hidden in their separate homes before the soldiers arrived. A widespread search would follow, and suspicion fall on any man who was not in his bed.

They helped the less badly wounded of their comrades from the spot; but dared not encumber themselves with those who were helpless.

Black George bent briefly over John, lying senseless beside Sam Hartley.

"Eh, lad!" was all he could find to say, but he brushed his sleeve across his face as someone dragged him away.

19

A Lark Singing

THERE WERE MANY that night who were harshly awakened from sleep by the strident call of the alarm bell. Some burrowed their heads deeper under the bedclothes, fearful of knowing what the signal might portend: others were frankly curious, and heads poked out of windows as neighbour exchanged surmise with neighbour. But when the noise of the bell was followed by the sound of scurrying footsteps through the villages; when, later, the clatter of mounted troops swept past beneath their windows; then the people of the district were in little doubt as to what had taken place.

Mary Lister guessed earlier than many, for the firing and shouting were plainly audible from the Vicarage. At first, she crouched wretchedly in her bed, listening and wondering anxiously how Arkwright was faring, for it was of him that she first thought. She did not seriously entertain the idea that her cousin might be one of the attackers. She knew his gentle spirit; and failed to allow sufficiently for the influence of George Mellor, and the binding effect of the Luddite oath.

After a time, she heard sounds of movement in the house, and went out on to the landing. Mrs. Duckworth stood there in a voluminous dressing-gown, a candle held in one shaking hand.

"What is it, Miss Mary?" she whispered, fearfully. "It sounds as though them black devils is attacking t' mill."

Mary admitted that this was what she, too, feared; and the two women agreed to dress and brew a comforting dish of tea downstairs in the kitchen.

It was while they were sipping this by the resuscitated fire that they heard the soldiers ride past. Mrs. Duckworth blenched.

"Pray Heaven Master John's not mixed up in this lot!" she said, feverently.

"I can't think it," replied Mary, attempting comfort. "You know his views on violence."

"Ay, but a good lad times gets led into evil by others—they know how to work on him."

This was so much what Arkwright had once said of John that Mary's heart missed a beat as she considered the likelihood again. Who could say what arguments might be brought to bear on her cousin? What threats, even? Then there was the solemn oath which she had heard him take—he was so young in experience, though intellectually ahead of his years.

She set down her cup, a sudden wave of panic sweeping over her. Mrs. Duckworth noticed the change in her face, and went to her side.

"Don't swoon, now, lass. Put thy head down, so——"

"I'm all right," said Mary, trying to rally herself. "It's the late hour, and the anxiety—and oh, I wish I could be there, and know for myself what is happening! It's the uncertainty that's so hard to bear."

"Get back to bed," urged the housekeeper, forgetting some of her own anxiety in the present need to care for someone else. "We can do no good, here, and we'll learn nowt till t' morning."

But Mary could not face the prospect of a darkened room alive with the bogies of her imagination. She chose to remain where she was, and the housekeeper stayed with her. They sat on by the leaping fire which could no longer warm them; talking and falling silent by turns, but always coming back to the one subject which occupied both minds.

It was after three o'clock when they heard a knock on the back door. They looked at each other in silent apprehension for a moment and made no attempt to answer it.

The knock was repeated, though not loudly. Mrs. Duckworth rose reluctantly to her feet, and, seizing the poker from the hearth, went over to the door. White-faced, Mary picked up the shovel and followed at her heels.

The housekeeper shot back the bolts, turned the key in the lock, and slowly opened the door.

"Don't be afraid." It was Arkwright, and he stepped at once into the room, closing the door after him. "I saw a chink of light under the door, and guessed some-one was astir."

Standing in the full light of the lamp, he startled them by his dishevelled appearance. His clothes were dirty and torn, his hands smeared with grease and grime, and there was a small jagged cut on his cheek on which the blood had dried.

"You're in a right pickle," said Mrs. Duckworth, surveying him. "Come in and sit you down, sir, and I'll get you a drop o' summat. You look as if you could do wi' it, an' all."

"Thank you, no time for that," replied Arkwright. He looked quickly from one to the other of them, inwardly dreading to break the news he brought, but giving no sign beyond a more than usual sternness of countenance. "I've bad news for you," he continued, abruptly. "Prepare yourselves for an unpleasant shock."

"It's John," said Mary, putting her hand to her mouth. "He's—he's dead?"

The words tailed away.

"Dying," answered Arkwright. "He can't last the night. That's why I've come for you. You must rouse your uncle, and break the news to him. There isn't much time, if he would see the lad before he goes."

"Oh, my lamb, my lamb, my baby!" Mrs. Duckworth was beside herself with grief. "How could the Lord let a sweet innocent like him suffer for the misdeeds of others? Oh, my little lad—so gentle, so kind!"

"Hush, dear," soothed Mary, putting her arms about the motherly form, while the tears dropped unheeded from her own eyes. "There, hush now."

"The Luddites made an attack on my mill tonight," explained Arkwright, avert'ng his eyes from their distress. "He was with them, and was wounded—shot in the leg. It's had to be amputated—he's under arrest, of course, but I persuaded them to get a surgeon to him. He's at the inn at Robertown. Colonel Grey's agreed for his father to see him—and you, if you desire it, ma'am"—his eyes turned to Mary for a brief moment—"no one else, I'm afraid."

Mrs. Duckworth dropped into a chair, and began to sob unrestrainedly.

"I'll go to my uncle at once," said Mary, white to the lips, but quite controlled. "I'll get him ready as soon as possible."

She lit a candle at the fire, and, leaving them together in the kitchen, groped her way, blind with tears, to the stairs. She must not break down now: later, perhaps, when all the sorry tale of the day was told—but not now. Her uncle and Mrs. Duckworth needed her support.

Sometimes, in later years, she would wake in the night crying out in torment at the memory of that next ten minutes when she was forced to give her uncle the news that broke his heart. In those days yet to come, there was one close by to comfort her on such occa-

sions with loving words, and to remind her not to rouse
the child who slumbered peacefully in the adjacent cot,
and who bore her cousin's name. Somehow, she managed to accomplish the dreaded task. After the first
anguished incredulity, her uncle found much that required an explanation, for he had been entirely ignorant of his son's activities. Her answers brought added
grief, as he realized how far apart their ways had lain
through the years since John had lost his mother.

"Mea culpa," he said, in deep sorrow. "I should
have shared my son's life, but I left him to manage it
alone. The blame is mine, but the punishment is
heavy."

He bent his head for a moment in prayer; then, having flung on some clothes, went downstairs with Mary
to join Arkwright.

In the small room at the inn to which the mill-owner
presently brought them, John Booth was lying inert on
a truckle bed, his face totally drained of colour and his
eyes closed. There was an odour of medicaments in the
room, heavily overlaid by the stench of blood. A wave
of nausea hit Mary's stomach as she entered; but she
fought it down, advancing to the bed alongside her
uncle.

"I'll do my best to see that you're left alone with
him," said Arkwright, placing chairs for them at the
bedside. "But he's under arrest, of course, and the
Colonel keeps trying to get out of him the names of
those who were with him in the attack—so far, without
success."

"How can he?" asked Mary, with tearful indignation. "How can he bring himself to pester a dying
man?"

He looked at her compassionately. "I'll try my best
to prevent any more of it. But you must realize how it
is—Colonel Grey's in command, here."

He left them. They sat there in silence for some
time, watching the white face with its deep lines of suffering, listening to the laboured breathing.

At last, John opened his eyes, and stared at them for
a moment without recognition. Then he looked straight
at his father with awareness, and spoke in a faint,

breathless voice that—strangely—never once held any
suggestion of a stutter.

"Father." He put out his hand, and the Vicar
clasped it firmly between his own trembling fingers.
"Can you—forgive—me?"

"It is I who need forgiveness, my son. How could I
have neglected you so—failed to gain your confidence?
I have not done my duty as a parent."

"They're too close, father—parents and children—
too close, yet too far apart———"

The old man shook his head, unable to speak.

"Don't grieve, father. There must be—some purpose———"

His voice tailed away, and for several moments he
said nothing more. Then he looked at Mary.

"Sam Hartley, too—they've got him in the next
room—he'll—he'll—not last long———" He took a deep,
gasping breath, and continued, "You'll not forget his
children? And—Arkwright———" his eyes watched her
face as though he would penetrate her thoughts—
"don't let—this—stand between you, Mary. I know
you—love him—he—did the best he could—for me—
even getting Colonel Grey—to let you both come———"

"Don't try to talk any more, love," said Mary,
gently. "Save your strength. I'll see that Sam's children
are all right—don't worry about anything, just now."

He managed a brief, twisted smile. "Remember—the
meadow where we played—when we were children?
One day, early—the sun was just rising—a lark
sang———"

She bent her head to hide the swift rush of tears.
Just then, the door opened, and Colonel Grey came
abruptly into the room, with Arkwright hard on his
heels, looking like thunder.

"Ah, he seems to be talking now, right enough,"
said the Colonel, by way of greeting. "Well, Booth, do
you mean to tell me who was with you in the raid? It
will ease your conscience, y'know—I'm sure you'll bear
me out there, Vicar?"

John's father turned a look of reproachful misery on
the Colonel. "Let my son die in peace, sir."

John spoke up from the bed, faintly but audibly. "Can you—keep a secret, Colonel?"

Colonel Grey assented eagerly, and drew nearer to the bed in case he should miss what followed.

John raised himself a little way on one elbow, and spoke in a stronger voice than he had so far used. "Well, so can I."

He relapsed exhausted on the pillow; his lips were blue, but they moved for a moment. Colonel Grey turned away angrily, but Mary and her uncle bent forward to catch the faint words.

"I can still hear the lark singing——"

The voice stopped abruptly. His head lolled sideways, like a broken doll's; a lock of fair hair fell across his brow.

The Vicar bent forward to kiss the lifeless face, and gently close the staring eyes. Then he dropped to his knees, to pray for the boy whose only crime had been a deep concern in the welfare of others.

They buried Sam Hartley at Halifax on the following Wednesday. Much to the surprise and concern of the authorities, a great concourse of people attended the funeral. Ugly rumours ran round the crowd; it was whispered that the two men had been tortured at Robertown in an abortive attempt to force them to betray their companions in the attack. Soldiers rode up and down to see that order was maintained, but there were no incidents.

It was clear, however, that hundreds of people could be expected again at John Booth's funeral, which was due to take place the next day. To avoid the undesirable publicity, with its attendant risks, the authorities insisted that the time of the funeral should be changed. Accordingly, it was held at first light: apart from John's own household and the military, only Arkwright and Nick Bradley stood bareheaded at the graveside.

"There's summat I must tell thee, Maister," said Nick, as they walked together through the dewy grass to the churchyard. "I can't keep it no longer to mysen, though happen tha'lt turn me off when tha knows all. I did it for t' poor lad's sake, but t'weren't no manner o' good, for he's dead now, just t' same."

"What are you speaking of?" asked Arkwright, coming out of his gloomy abstraction. "What did you do?"

Somewhat shamefacedly, Nick explained how he had gone to the Vicarage to try and prevent John from attending the meeting at the St. Crispin, and what had followed when he had told Mary of the impending raid on the inn.

"I know what tha's thinking," concluded Nick. "And happen I'd think same, in thy place. But yon poor lass had enough to bear, then, wi'out finding her cousin in trouble, too. But if tha feels, Maister Will——" his voice shook a little—"that tha's no use for a man who'd turn traitor after all these years, well——"

"So that's what happened," said Arkwright. "I knew there must be somebody; but I never thought of you, of course."

The overseer winced. "Dost want me to go, lad? I don't blame thee——"

Arkwright's mouth twisted as though in pain. "No, Nick. I would have saved the boy, too, if I could have done—for his own sake, partly, but much more for her sake. I don't blame you—who knows? I might have done the same thing, had I been you."

They said no more then, for they had arrived at the spot where the other mourners stood. Arkwright glanced covertly at Mary, a small, grey figure merging mournfully into the grey of the early morning light. A deep black band encircled her arm to speak of her loss. Once only did their eyes meet; on that occasion, it was as though she looked straight through him.

"——In Whom whosoever believeth shall live, though he die——"

The words floated tremulously across the new-dug grave. Far above the bowed heads gathered round it, the first red streaks of the rising sun broke the dullness of the sky; and a lark's song was clearly heard.

20

To Build Jerusalem

IN THE DAYS that followed, Mary forgot her own sorrow in trying to bring comfort to her uncle and Mrs. Duckworth. She knew that presently they would recover their tranquillity in finding something to do for others; but for the moment she abandoned all idea of returning to her own home.

She had not forgotten her promise to John, and at the first opportunity visited the Hartleys' cottage. A neighbour told her that the children had been taken in by Jack Hartley's wife, who lived some distance away.

" 'Twill mean short commons, I reckon, ma'am, especially now poor Jack's been taken afore t' military on account o' not firin' on his own brother in t' riot. They say Maister Arkwright's to give evidence agin him at t' trial—no wonder folks call him Bloodhound."

A spasm of pain crossed Mary's face. She asked to be directed to Jack Hartley's dwelling, and found it was too far away for her to visit at that time. When she returned home, she settled with Mrs. Duckworth that they should both go there on the following afternoon.

"Though I don't quite know how I can help," she said, unhappily. "It's money they need, and there I am powerless to assist. By the way, the woman told me that Sally—the eldest girl—has found a situation with the doctor's wife."

"That will be one less mouth to feed," said the housekeeper. "I wonder who spoke for the lass?"

Mary shook her head. "I don't know. But it seems hard for a child of ten to be slaving away in someone's kitchen—she should be in the schoolroom——"

"Labourers' children lead different lives from them

as you teach, Miss Mary. But *he* would've thought like that——" Her eyes filled with tears.

"If I could find another post hereabouts," said Mary slowly, "I might perhaps be able to start a Sunday school, and teach some of the labouring children to read. He would have wanted that——"

"I thought you'd decided to go away? Not that your uncle and me wouldn't bless the day, if you stayed on——"

Mary coloured. "When I said that, I was only thinking of myself. I wanted to put as much distance as possible between myself and—and——"

"And Mr. Arkwright?" hazarded the housekeeper shrewdly.

Mary nodded. "But now I wonder if there isn't work for me to do here. John's life must not have been in vain. The things he believed in—he said there was a purpose. Perhaps this is it."

"Happen you'd find something in Halifax. But you'd need a reference from your last post. I suppose Mr. Arkwright——"

"I shall ask no favours of him."

On the following morning, Mrs. Arkwright called at the Vicarage, accompanied by Caroline. While her mother talked gently to the Vicar of his dead son, Caroline plied Mary with eager questions.

"Why would you not return to us, Miss Lister? Will says he begged you to come back, but you would not."

"He did not exactly beg," answered Mary dryly.

"Oh, that is just his manner! But I know he wanted you to, and so do I. I miss you dreadfully."

"I miss you, too, Caroline. But it would not answer—I seem to have a particular knack of annoying your brother."

"You don't understand, ma'am—it's because he likes you so much. I know he does sometimes fly into a passion, but he is the dearest, kindest creature at heart!"

Mary abruptly changed the subject by asking how Caroline was getting on with her music. The girl shook her head, and said it was difficult to make any progress without a teacher's guiding hand.

"I suppose you couldn't—but no, of course I must not ask!" she finished, with a guilty expression.

Mary pressed her to explain.

"I was wondering if you could come and hear me play sometimes. Just now and then, you know—when Will isn't there, of course——"

Mary hesitated. She could never again enter Arkwright's employment, but was there any reason why she should not visit his house as Caroline's friend? The child had real musical talent, and it was a pity to neglect it.

In the end, she agreed, and found herself bound to an engagement for the very next morning.

As they were leaving, Mrs. Arkwright, with some evident embarrassment, pressed a package into Mary's hand. Once they had gone, she opened it.

She found banknotes to the value of ten pounds, and a curt note from Arkwright indicating that this was six months' salary in lieu of notice.

Her cheeks flamed. For a moment, she determined to return it all with a disdainful reply. Then she realized that she could not do this: she must give Mrs. Duckworth something for her board, and her own mother needed help, too. Besides, some of it at least had already been earned. Mature consideration decided her to keep this amount, and to give the balance to Sam Hartley's family, whom she was visiting that afternoon.

She and Mrs. Duckworth found the cottage without difficulty, and were invited into a room crammed with children, many of them busy about simple household tasks. Mrs. Hartley seemed a sensible woman, but she was evidently in some distress at present. She explained that this was because her husband's court martial had taken place today, and she was anxiously awaiting the result.

"Maister Arkwright's to bring word on his way back home, ma'am. He called in early this mornin' afore he went, to tell me as he meant to put in a strong plea for mercy, things bein' as they was, wi' Sam Jack's brother, an' all."

"A plea for mercy?" asked Mary. "That isn't what we were told."

"There's not many knows it; an' I don't mind tellin' thee, ma'am, as it come as a surprise to me, too. My Jack won't hear a word agin Maister Arkwright, but I've always reckoned 'im a 'ard man, an' I made sure he'd stand out for Jack bein' punished. But no—he said this mornin' as Jack's a loyal worker—which is no more'n t' truth—so he meant to stand by him. Please God they'll hearken to him, or what'll become on us?"

This led Mary on to speak of the money. Mrs. Hartley said little, but the tears ran down her face as she accepted it. Mrs. Duckworth cautioned her to make it last, and congratulated her on Sally's having found work.

"Ay. 'Twas Maister Arkwright as spoke up for her there," said the woman, wiping her eyes.

"He's got a finger in most pies, seemingly," replied the housekeeper. "I hear they're calling him Bloodhound roundabout."

"Ay—since t' funeral. Poor young John Booth, ma'am——" she turned to Mary. "We were all very sorry—he was thought a deal of. But we don't know what to mak' on Maister Arkwright lately, an' that's a fact. Reckon he's changed."

There seemed nothing more to say, so they prepared to take their leave. As they stood at the door, they were startled by the sound of firing close at hand, and a moment later, a rider came at full gallop round the bend. He drew up at the cottage door, and slid from his sweating horse. They saw it was Arkwright.

"Maister Arkwright! For Lord's sake, what's amiss?" cried Mrs. Hartley.

"Someone took a pot shot at me." Mary saw that there was blood streaming down his face. "Can you give me something to clean this up? Better not let your children see me in this state—I'll go round to the pump."

Mary had turned white, but she took the horse's reins from him. "You're hurt, sir. You'd best sit down while we see if it's serious."

He glanced keenly at her. "Nonsense—it's only a

graze, you know. Thank God he was a poor shot. I'll see to it myself—some linen, please, Mrs. Hartley."

A bundle of clean rag was provided, and in spite of protests he went alone to the pump at the back of the cottage.

When he returned, he had wiped the blood from his face, and wore his hat at a rakish angle to conceal his improvised bandage beneath.

"All's right," he declared. "At least I shan't frighten my people out of their wits when I appear at the door."

"But who could have done it?" asked Mary. "Will you try and find the culprit?"

"I think not—he did his best to find me, and next time he might succeed. He's armed—I'm not."

He turned to Mrs. Hartley. "I'm sorry for the news I must bring. My plea was refused—Jack's to be sent to the mill tomorrow morning to be flogged in punishment of his disobedience."

The women cried out in horror, and Mrs. Hartley began to sob.

"Don't take on," he said gently, laying a hand on her arm. "I'll find a way—trust me. I must go now."

He took the reins from Mary's hands, and swinging into the saddle, rode away.

When Arkwright arrived at the mill the next morning, he found a large crowd assembled. Although a public execution of the sentence had been ordered by the authorities, he had hoped that in fact few people other than the Militia, whose attendance was compulsory, would appear. He had failed to win a reprieve for the man, and must see that the sentence was carried out unless he wished to fall foul of the authorities himself. The only concession he had been able to win was that the severity of the sentence should be left to his own discretion. Not for the first time, he cursed the chance that had taken Colonel Grey to the mill on the night of the attack: without his presence there, this need never have happened.

The crowd continued to grow, until by the appointed hour it numbered several hundreds. Arkwright reflected that if riots should begin, it would not be easy to subdue them with the small force of military present. Moreover, there were no reserves, for they had been withdrawn to another part of the West Riding following the welcome peace which had fallen over the neighbourhood since the attack.

Prompt to the minute, the escort arrived with their manacled prisoner; a handful of them, in charge of a sergeant whose business it would be to carry out the flogging. They saluted Arkwright, and set about their business with military efficiency.

The crowd, which had frozen into immobility at the first appearance of the soldiers, now began to stir and murmur. Here and there, a barely perceptible signal passed round among them, and a few of their number slipped unobtrusively away. None of this was noticed by Arkwright and the military, as they were busy with the prisoner.

He was being stripped to the waist and tied to one of the gateposts. When he was ready, the sergeant stood over him and slowly raised the wicked-looking whip.

His first stroke had no bite to it: this particular man always took time to warm to his work. It fell about the prisoner's shoulders almost as a caress.

But today he was not to be given time to get into his stride. Even as he drew back the whip to raise it for a second stroke, the order rang sharply out: "Stop!"

He paused, lowering the lash, a puzzled expression on his stolid face.

"It is over," stated Arkwright, whose voice had shouted the command. "The sentence has been carried out. Release the prisoner."

The sergeant opened his mouth to protest, thought better of it, saluted smartly, and sprang to obey.

The crowd went mad. Hats were flung into the air, cheers rang out, and some started to dance and sing. Arkwright paid no heed, but went to Jack Hartley and helped him into his shirt.

"I'd no choice, lad," he said. "It had to be done, but I'd the right to stop it when I chose."

Hartley nodded, his face working. He could not have

spoken, even had there been any chance of making himself heard in all that hullabaloo.

"Get out of this into the mill," shouted Arkwright. "We'll get you home after the crowd disperses."

Hartley tried to obey, but the excited crowd pressed round him, trying to hoist him on their shoulders, in spite of his protests.

Arkwright turned away to dismiss the escort and the Militia. They went readily enough, the escort still looking as though they could not believe what had happened.

He then made one or two attempts to dismiss the crowd; but it was in high holiday spirits, and at last he gave up, pushing his way through in the direction of the mill door.

He had almost reached it when he felt a sharp tug on his sleeve, and turning, saw Nick Bradley trying to come close enough to him for speech. The overseer's face was full of alarm.

"Maister Will! Some on 'em's gone to t' house, to break in!"

Arkwright seized him roughly. "What do you mean?"

"I've just heard tell—there's some left here afore t' flogging began—they don't know tha stopped it, an' they mean to avenge Jack! For God's sake, mak' haste! There's Miss Caro an'——"

"Come on!"

Side by side they fought their way ruthlessly through the crowd until they managed to win clear. They began to race along the path that led to the house.

The noise of the crowd gradually receded; as it did, other more ominous noises reached their ears. Shouts and jeers floated across the distance; as Arkwright made a last, desperate spurt and burst through the shrubbery, there was a sudden crash of breaking glass.

He paused for a second only as he reached the drive, surveying the scene. The attackers numbered about a score. Most of them were battering on the door of the house with sticks and other handy implements. They kept up a constant stream of abuse which was answered freely by the domestics from within. Arkwright identified easily the strident, defiant tones of Nellie's voice.

Several windows were broken. He saw a man climb up to one on the ground floor, and throw his leg over the sill, about to enter the room beyond.

At the same moment, a shrill scream rang out. It was Caroline's voice.

He rushed forward, his feet scarcely seeming to touch the ground. He managed to reach the window before he was noticed. By now, the man had entered the room; just as Arkwright was about to follow him, a shout arose, and he was seized from behind.

He turned, and aimed a couple of punishing blows at his assailant. The man grunted and doubled up, but by now others had rushed to take his place. With his back to the window, Arkwright gave fight.

Occupied as he was with four or five opponents, he could hear sounds of a sharp scuffle taking place in the room behind, and several screams rang out. The thought of what might be happening in there maddened him so that he could scarcely see his attackers' faces, but it lent fury to his blows. He fought like one possessed.

Nick Bradley had been outpaced by his more virile master, and had only now arrived on the scene. He saw at once how matters stood, and rushed to Arkwright's aid.

"For God's sake, stop!" he shouted, as he ran. "Ye're making a mistake—he stopped t' floggin', I tell ye—Jack's none t' worse——"

But no one listened. Instead, they rushed upon him, and soon he was in the thick of the fight.

Arkwright was flagging. He was oblivious now of the sounds from the room behind him, and did not notice a sudden crash of shattering china, or the silence that followed this. But he did hear a woman's voice ring out in a desperate appeal, and knew that it was Mary's.

"Stop—for the love of God, stop! Hasn't there been bloodshed enough—my cousin's life, and the lives of those you love, too—isn't it enough? Oh, stop, I implore you—before it's too late!"

"Hold tha noise, woman!" One of Arkwright's opponents shouted contemptuously. "Dost think we'll listen to thee?"

"But you will listen to me."

The clear, compelling voice sounded above all the hubbub, carrying with it the age-old authority of the Church. "In God's name, I command you to cease fighting. From this moment, any man who raises his hand against another will be accursed."

Hands dropped to sides, and a deep silence fell. Few men there were deeply religious, yet the solemn warning struck at the instinctive fear of them all.

They stared up at the man who sat with quiet dignity astride an old cob. He was bareheaded, his white hair gleaming in the sun: he looked to them like one of the old prophets.

He began to preach. It was no scholarly sermon on an obscure text such as he was wont to give his congregations. This time, he spoke of their daily problems from his heart, and found a ready echo in their own.

He spoke of the hatred and violence that had lately been abroad among them, and of the sorrowful harvest it had brought. While he talked, his listeners gradually grew in numbers, augmented by members of the crowd which was now dispersing from the mill. They had come to carry Jack in triumph to the house not caring in their high spirits that neither he nor Arkwright desired such a display. As they reached the spot, their laughter died away. Some were hushed by others: soon all stood listening to the solemn tones of that powerful voice.

"I could talk to you of patience and humility, for we all have need of these Christian virtues. But since my son's death———" the voice wavered for a second, then regained its firmness—"I have come to see that there is a new spirit abroad among men that will not rest until a better world has been made for all people here below. But it is not through hatred and conflict between men and master that such a world will be built. If you would make Jerusalem in England's green and pleasant land, it must be shoulder to shoulder, with each ready to give his utmost for a common cause. If both master and men will realize that they share a common humanity in God, then though there be disagreements, a way can be found to reconcile them."

He paused, looking about him. Everyone was motionless. He saw that Arkwright, almost exhausted, was leaning against the window frame above which the heads of some womenfolk—his own dear Mary's among them—had appeared.

"It is not an easy counsel that I give you," he continued. "It is easy to hate, and to act violently. But that is the way of a child, and ye are men. As men, then, go forward to grapple with the problems that beset you, and God be your guide. As for what has happened here today, it is best forgotten, except as a warning to you all. I call upon your employer to set you an example in the way of life I would have you follow. What say you, Mr. Arkwright? Will you agree to overlook what has taken place?"

Arkwright suddenly found himself the focus of all eyes. Fatigued though he was, he straightened, and made his voice heard.

"I will do as you ask, Vicar. There are no easy solutions to our problems, as you say. I believe that we are on the brink of an age when machines will play an increasing part in our lives, and we must learn to adapt ourselves accordingly. Strife achieves nothing: in future I and my workmen must try to talk over changes, and see what we can arrive at by agreement."

A prolonged cheer went up, and the crowd showed signs of breaking out into high spirits once again. But the Vicar held up a hand for silence, and a hush fell over them all.

"There has been excitement enough for one day, and most of you are sorely in need of rest and quiet. Go, then, peaceably to your homes, and never forget what has been said here today. And the blessing of God Almighty go with you, and remain with you always."

21

Reconciliation

EARLY IN THE evening of the same day, Mary was sitting alone in the Vicarage parlour. She was trying to read, but her thoughts strayed constantly from the page before her. She gave it up at last, and went to the window, gazing out abstractedly at the daffodils which had only recently come into bloom. Spring was here at last with its delicate beauty and promise of brighter days in store; but its hopeful message did not find an echo in her own heart.

She looked up on hearing the click of the latch as the gate opened: a man entered, and began to walk to the house. Her pulses gave a sudden leap as she recognized William Arkwright. He noticed her before she had time to draw back from the window, and signaled to her.

She went to the door, and opened it to him. Then she hesitated, uncertain whether or not to invite him inside. Her uncle was out at present, and she could not suppose that Arkwright would wish to see her, after all that had previously passed between them.

"Do you wish to see my uncle?" she asked. "I'm afraid he's over at the church. I don't quite know when he will return, but you will find him there—unless you care to wait?"

"No," he answered, abruptly.

"You won't wait?"

"Not that." It struck her now that he was far from being at ease himself. "I meant that I didn't come to see the Vicar. I came to see you."

"Oh——"

"May I come in? We cannot very well talk here."

She blushed. "I beg your pardon. Yes, of course."

She showed him into the parlour, and asked him to sit down. He took a chair, but almost immediately stood up again.

"I suppose you may wonder——" he began, then broke off. "I trust you feel all right after this morning's ordeal?" he asked, in a brisker tone. "Perhaps you are not yet up to visitors—should you like me to call another time?"

"Oh, no! That is to say—yes, I feel perfectly all right, thank you."

She stole a glance at him. His face bore the marks of the violent scenes through which he had recently passed. There was a small scar on his right cheek, a plaster on his forehead, and a faint bruising round his left eye. His expression was that of a small boy paying some tiresome and acutely embarrassing call of civility.

A sudden wave of maternal tenderness swept over Mary. No doubt he had called to ask after her health as a gesture that he wished them to part friends. She had returned home with her uncle this morning soon after the crowd had dispersed, and there had been no time to say more than goodbye. Arkwright had been too occupied with the business of setting his house to rights.

She determined to make his mission easier.

"It was good of you to call," she said, with more warmth in her manner. "But I am perfectly recovered, as you see. I trust that Mrs. Arkwright and Caroline are none the worse?"

He shook his head. "They're both resilient people—like you," he said. "Caroline told me how you managed to dispose of the fellow who tried to attack all three of you, this morning."

There was a faintly humorous tone in his voice.

"I did not at all like it when he fell to the ground," said Mary, with a shudder. "I feared at first I had killed him. But he grabbed Caroline, and was hurting her, although she scratched him like anything——"

"I'll wager she would!"

"She was really terrified, though, and Mrs. Arkwright and I were not strong enough to fight him off. So I picked up that large vase, and hit him on the head. I hope it was not a valuable one," she added, as an afterthought.

"It was. But don't let that disturb you—I never could stand the sight of it." He gave a grim smile. "You can always think of something to do, can't you? I believe you must be the most resourceful person I have ever met."

There seemed to be nothing to say to this, so she kept silent. He gave her an intent look.

"May I ask what are your plans for the future?"

"I don't really know. I must find another post presently; but for the moment, I feel I cannot leave my uncle."

He nodded, and fell silent, staring out of the window. Mary searched her brain frantically, but could think of nothing else to say on her part.

He turned suddenly, and faced her with a determined look.

"Do you mean to marry Arthur Webster?" he asked abruptly.

She was taken aback. Nothing had led her to expect the question, and she felt it as an impertinence.

"I have not had the honour of being asked," she answered, in reproving accents.

"But if you were—what would you say?"

There was a moment's silence.

"I think that is my concern, Mr. Arkwright."

"Yes—but it's mine, too. Do you—I must know— are you—in love with the fellow?"

She looked at him in amazement, then she began to laugh.

"Well! Really, I cannot imagine what business it is of yours, sir!"

"Can't you?" His eyes held hers for a moment. "You must be more stupid than I think you, then. Come—I need an answer."

"And I don't intend to give you one. I've told you before that you cannot take that tone with me."

"You really are the most provoking——"

He broke off, and seized her by the elbows in the way he had done on the occasion of their last meeting in this room. "I tell you I will have an answer, if I have to shake it out of you!"

"Let me go!" She struggled to free herself. "You are too ready to lay your hands on me, and I dislike it excessively!"

"You may have to accustom yourself to it," he said, grimly, but he released her.

"I'm sure I don't know what you mean," she said, but this was by now not strictly true.

"No? Well, we'll let that pass for the moment. Mary, I want you to listen to me—seriously."

She was finding some difficulty in breathing at a normal rate, but she appeared calm enough to his eyes.

"I don't know how to begin—I've no skill in this kind of thing——"

"What kind of thing?" It was unpardonable of her, but she was teasing him.

"Oh, damn it all!" He gave an impatient gesture. "Listen—before you came to Liversedge, I was alone. I had my work, and I had nothing else—it occupied all my thoughts, and I could share my responsibilities with no one else. I told you this once before, recollect."

She nodded, more sober now.

"Then you came," he continued. "I felt at once I could confide in you, even rely on you——"

"That is not the impression you gave me." Mary could not help interrupting him at this remark. "You made me feel sadly inadequate at times."

"You are thinking of that business with Caroline? I realized afterwards that you were perfectly right, and that I was expecting too much of you, if you were supposed to know what she was about every moment or her day. But at the time, my anxiety for her overruled all considerations of the kind——"

"I see," said Mary. "And I suppose it was the same kind of thing that led you to think the worst of me over the threatening letter? That hardly suggested that you placed any reliance in me, you know."

He looked a trifle taken aback. "Yes, well, you must see how it was—that note had put me in a passion, and my judgment was distorted. Afterwards, of course——"

"I see. So you feel you can rely on me—when you are not in a passion, sir?"

He looked at her severely. "I shall most certainly box your ears, one of these days. Take warning."

She moved away from him hastily.

"Mary," he continued, in a different tone. "I don't want to go on alone any more. All that I promised your uncle this morning—and much more, that I mean to attempt in my manufactory—I can't do it on my own. I need your help, lass." He paused. "It won't be an easy life. There's not too much money; and don't make the mistake of thinking that the labour troubles are all at an end—I certainly don't. There'll be outbreaks again, no doubt, though perhaps we shall have peace for a while, now. But we'll have hope, Mary— the hope of building up a secure business that will provide a living not only for us, but for hundreds of working folk: the hope of making a better world, as your uncle said this morning: the hope of a full life together."

He stopped suddenly, and moved closer to her, his eyes intense with feeling.

"So now you see why I must know whether you are in love with young Webster."

She shook her head. "I can't think why you should ever have supposed it."

"Well," he said, hesitantly. "It did seem that night as though you were enjoying his company."

"Just as you were enjoying Miss Grey's?"

"Oh, Miss Grey!" He shrugged. "She chose to amuse herself with me, that is all. She has found someone else for the honour, now."

"And so you turn to me?"

"There's no doubt about it, I shall have to box your ears! But don't tease me, Mary! Will you take me?"

"That depends. You've offered me many things, sir, but not the one I wanted."

He looked at her questioningly. "What more is there that I can offer?"

She looked down. "You've—you've said no word of love," she mentioned, "except in connection with Mr. Webster."

"Didn't you know?" he asked incredulously. "Didn't you ever guess?"

"No." She looked up with a shy smile. "I thought I was to accept you because you needed my help, and felt you could rely on me—when you weren't in a passion, of course——"

"Words are no use," he said, with difficulty. "Tell me one thing, first—do you care for me at all?"

"Didn't you know?" she mimicked, softly. "Didn't you ever guess?"

"And you don't really dislike me to lay hands on you, as you said a while back?"

But she could not answer this. He looked into her face, and made up his mind.

"That's all I need to know," he said.